Maggie for Hire

By Kate Danley

To My Scooby Crew

and

Those Bloggers of the Golden Age

Chapter 1

I'm a tracker. Actually, my business card reads "Maggie MacKay - Magical Tracker". I find the bad guys and bring them in. And right now, I was getting the shit kicked out of me. It's a crummy job and, unfortunately, it's mine.

I appear to be a normal, thirty-something, Irish brunette. You know. With a penchant for bike leathers and, at this particular moment, wrestling vampires.

God, they stink. The whole undead process does not slow the rotting corpse action.

I had a trace on this one since he crawled out of the sewer to sit in the church eaves, hell- bent on taking out a couple of nice old nuns. I may not have all my priorities straight, but those ladies gave up getting laid to feed the hungry and care for the poor. You don't make gals like that lunch.

I had chased this sucker down a blind alley, silver stake in my hand. Unnecessarily fancy weaponry? Yes. You are correct. To kill a vampire, you just need a stake, anything pointy will do, but I never know what I'll be tracking next, so I try to go for multipurpose tools. Plus, my sister got this one engraved for me at *Things Remembered* last Christmas, which, I think, gives it some added class.

"Come on, would you just die already?" I grunted as he grappled with me, trying to get his fangs in my neck. I'd learned a long time ago to wear neckguards. Vampires will go for anywhere you've got a pulse, but it's when they get you in the neck that you have to worry.

"You are the one who will die!" he whispered, flipping me on my stomach and sitting on my back.

Crap. Not good.

"I have been waiting a long time to destroy you, Ms. MacKay."

Now, I might not be the swiftest boat in the fleet, but A) This guy shouldn't know my name and B) what's with the whole "long time to destroy me" action? I figured if I was potentially going to snuff it, I should at least ask. Between elbow punches to his ribcage as I tried to wriggle away, I managed to grunt out, "How do you know me?"

"I am afraid you are the one with the bounty upon her head."

"What does that even mean?"

I felt him fumbling with the locks on my guard. I was not about to have any of this. I grabbed him around the neck to roll him when I heard a THWACK and felt him stiffen, then fall off me. He landed, his wide eyes frozen upon my face.

I sat up.

"It appeared that you were in need of assistance."

My knight in shining armor was tall, easily 6'4, maybe 6'5, and impossibly gorgeous. The kind of guy you feel like you needed to apologize to afterwards for kissing because your face was unworthy of those lips. Lord almighty. He was slender and chiseled, golden locks tumbling around his merry blue eyes. Oh, and pointy ears, which explained the whole unearthly beauty. He was an elf. And evidently on my side. For the moment.

"Naw, I had him," I said, standing up and brushing off my pants. I so had NOT had him and a very terrified part of me didn't want to admit how close I had been to being a blood bank bento box just a couple minutes ago. "But, you know, thanks for saving me some time."

I picked up the vampire's arms and started dragging him down the alley.

"Permit me to assist you, fair lady."

I rolled my eyes. That's the deal with elves. Gorgeous. Mind-blowingly good lays. But you had to put up with the ridiculously archaic crap that came shooting out of their mouth. Still, he was stronger than me and I have no pride when it comes to getting out of moving dead weight.

"Eh, sure," I dropped the vampire with a thunk.

The elf picked the evil undead monster up like he was a two-pound kitten. Mrrrow.

"So, um… my car is over there," I said, pointed to a beat up Honda Civic sitting by the curb. "Just throw him in the trunk and I can give you a lift wherever you need to go."

"Actually, fair lady, my business is with you."

"Riiiight. Any hints?" I asked.

"I have a proposition for future employment."

Now, that's more like it. Business had been slow recently. I operated in Los Angeles, the city of broken dreams and assorted crap. There are millions of folks over here, each of them with huge imaginations and no outlet. It tends to attract a certain crowd from the Other Side. And when I say Other Side, I'm not talking about Brentwood.

There is this whole alternate world that exists in the same place, just a separate plane of existence, as the world that most humans know. There are some gifted folks, like my mom, that can see in between these planes and figure out how one world is going to screw with the other (because that's what we do). For every push on Earth, there is a pull on the Other Side. Normally, the two worlds stay happily on their respective planes, but sometimes the veil is kinda thin. It happens when things get out of whack, and let me tell you something, there is nothing balanced about Los Angeles. It is life lived with the volume cranked to 11 and with that much energy being put out, it's like a light to a moth - except these moths are seven-feet tall and will eat your face.

That's not to say the Other Side is filled with only monsters. Hell, I live there. There are some pretty good folks and sometimes they come over to Earth for a nice little staycation. Central Casting has a field day when the circus comes to town. All the movie monster extras you need, no prosthetics required!

But, unfortunately, I don't get to deal with those dudes. I get to deal with the scum of the magical world. Vampires, werewolves, trolls, you name it. If it is gross and wants to kill somebody, that's where I come in. It's my job to haul them back to the Other Side - undead or alive.

I popped the trunk and stood appreciatively as the elf dumped the V-pire amidst my spare tire and crossbow.

"A job, huh?"

The elf nodded.

"What did you say your name was?"

"Killian, at your command."

He bowed deeply, giving me a good look at

his muscular back. I could think of a couple of commands but none of them were appropriate within 500 feet of a church.

"Right. Hop in. We'll talk," I said as I slid behind the wheel, the car dinging at me insistently to buckle up my seatbelt. "So, what's this job?"

And that's when my car felt like it had been hit by a freight train.

"Hang on!" Killian cried.

Chapter 2

"WHAT THE FUCK!" I screamed as I grabbed the wheel.

Killian reached over and covered me with his body as the windows exploded.

The car rolled, air bags deployed, and we tumbled ass-over-teakettle, spare change and Kleenex boxes ricocheting around us.

Note to self, clean out car prior to next magical attack.

And then, just like that, it was done. I looked over at Killian as we hung upside down from our seatbelts.

"This is what I am here to see you about," he said.

"I'm out."

I unbuckled my seatbelt and fell to the roof that was now the floor of my car. I climbed through where my driver's side window should have been and stumbled to my feet.

"I'm out. The answer is no. Leave. Now."

Sirens wailed in the distance. Killian unbuckled himself and did the fall-and-crawl, "You are the only one I can turn to."

"Listen, my car has been destroyed by an invisible something and the cops are right around the corner. There is no way I can talk my way out of that vampire stuck in my trunk."

Human police get a little cranky when they toss your car and find a corpse.

Killian looked over at my smashed vehicle, silver blood oozing out the back, sirens coming closer. I saw him breathe in and make a decision before turning to me, "How badly do you want me to fix it?"

Oh no. No. No. No.

"You fucking elf. Don't you dare even pretend like you are about to bargain for a favor."

"I already saved your life," he said.

"You already did shit. You almost got me killed! I'm not binding myself to you!"

He opened his arms, palms up, "Just say the words and I can make this all go away."

Shit shit shit shit shit. Those elves don't spend all those extra years in the Other Side learning how to play nice, I'll tell you that much. I gripped my hair in my hands, only too aware of the warm sticky blood gushing from my scalp.

People couldn't know about me. They

couldn't know about what I did. If the folks on Earth got so much as a clue, I could have my license to travel between worlds pulled and be stuck spending the rest of my life in an asylum or pulling drinks at Starbucks. SHIT.

I could see the lights of the cop car now. Killian tilted his head, "Trust me."

"Trust you. TRUST YOU OFF A CLIFF. Fine, motherfucker, you've got it! I bind myself to you. In return for this favor, I owe you one favor. Fix this!"

Killian snapped his fingers and immediately a maelstrom of air was whipping around me. I saw the car right itself, the dents fill out, the windows re-grow. The pain of the cuts on my arms and my head healed without even the slightest hint of a scar. As the wind died, it was like nothing had ever happened.

The cop car slowed and the window rolled down. The hunkiest officer a single girl ever laid eyes on leaned out. I can't believe I gave up a portion of my soul to an elf when I could have been frisked and handcuffed by this guy. This was not my day.

"We heard that a woman was being attacked..."

Killian came over and draped his arms across my shoulders, "My lady and I have not borne witness to any disagreements."

The officer gave Killian a long look before talking to his partner, "Keep driving. Maybe they're up ahead."

Killian gave him a neighborly wave as they drove away.

I looked up at him, "If I could get away with killing you, you would be dead right now."

Killian smiled, "You should get in line."

Chapter 3

"We should discuss your debt," said Killian as he stared out at the lights on La Brea Blvd.

We were back in the car, headed for the border. Massive paranormal attack or not, I had the body of the dead undead in my trunk and I really wanted the storage space back.

"You're right and you have no idea the joy that bubbleth over when I think upon our upcoming fireside chat," I said, opening up the console next to my seat. "But I gotta get this guy dropped off in order to pick up my finder's fee. Color me crazy, I'm not so good at multitasking when it comes to fighting for my life and covering my rent."

"I could get you there faster," Killian said with a wicked little glint in his eye.

"You greedy bastard, I owe you one mark already, I'm not going down that road for more. Jesus, you elves are all the frickin' same."

"Human favors are things of beauty."

"Yah, yah..."

"You are a thing of beauty..."

"Can it, elf, or I will crush your summer fruit into a nice dinner wine."

He smiled.

I fucking hate elves.

"Listen," I said, flipping a couple switches on the dashboard. "The border is coming up quick and I won't be distracted by you or anyone else. Got it?"

Killian settled back into his seat and made the universal sign for "after you". I gave him the universal sign for "up yours, buddy".

The car hit 45 mph on the winding back roads of Mulholland. Ex-mobster mansions are tucked into the sandy hills, their winding driveways barely visible in between the scrub brush and cacti. LA, evidently, ran out of money for guardrails and upkeep, though. The road is filled with potholes and the shoulder drops off sharply to canyons below. We sped past a scenic lookout where, on a clear day, you can see the Hollywood sign on one side and the ocean on the other. On a bad day, all you can see is smog.

But tonight, the air was clear and warm; the kind of night where you don't know where your body ends and the world begins. I pressed my foot to the floor and hit 70 on the hairpin turn. We drove off the edge of the cliff and soared out into the open sky.

Chapter 4

The car hit the ground with a thud.

"Crap. Traffic."

It was bumper-to-bumper in the Other Side.

The Other Side is pretty much every old book you've ever read come to life, settled in nice and cozy to the conveniences of modern living. If you can imagine it, it probably exists over here. The neighborhood we landed in had a particularly Victorian flair - cobblestone streets and Dickens-esque shops, bustle wearing bonneted ladies walking alongside the monsters of your nightmares.

We crept along to the backside of the police station. A blue woman, and not in the emotional kind of way, an actual blue woman, came out and I popped my trunk. She was flanked by two zombie porters.

"Nice one, Maggie. Next time, try not to kill 'em, okay?"

"Lacy, he's a vampire. He was already dead. I

just finished the job."

She shook her head at me and then noticed Killian in my passenger seat. "Well, well, well...," she purred, "Who's the six-pack-of-awesome-going-on-under-the-silken-tunic sitting there in your car?"

I think I sprained my eyeballs rolling them so hard, "He's a fucking elf. And he wants me to do a job for him."

Lacy clucked her tongue, "You could do worse."

"No," I said, slamming the trunk closed after the zombies lifted the vampire skip out. "No, I don't think I could."

"Listen, honey..." Lacy interrupted herself to shout at the zombie porter, "Cut it out! He's a vampire! He doesn't have a brain!"

The porter removed his mouth from the vampire's temple and continued to carry the carcass into the station.

Lacy shook her head, "The work ethic these days..."

I gave her a sympathetic shrug, hoping if I appeared to look like I cared, she'd finish the paperwork faster.

She ripped off the receipt, "Here you go."

I smiled and tucked it into my jacket pocket.

"Check will be in the mail."

"Thanks," I said, climbing back into my car.

Lacy leaned inside my window, "Listen, honey, you be careful, you hear? Rumor has it you've pissed off a bunch of people."

"Lacy, I know what I'm doing," I said. "Just keep the work rolling in. I can handle it."

I gave her a little finger wave as I backed out.

"You cannot handle it," said Killian.

"Yes, I can," I said, my knuckles turning white on the steering wheel.

Chapter 5

I opened up the door to my apartment, keys jingling in the door. My huge, orange tabby, Mac, came running up to me with sweet little "brrrows" of hello. I scooped him up and buried my face in his fur. There was nothing in the world this guy couldn't fix.

I walked into the center of the room and set him down, flinging my bag on the floor and kicking off my shoes.

"Can I get you anything to drink?" I asked Killian as I walked towards the kitchen to get Mac his dinner.

"Ambrosia nectar?"

"How about a beer?"

"That would also be acceptable."

I grabbed a couple longnecks from the fridge and popped the caps, handing one to Killian.

I stepped back into the kitchen and sucked mine down as quick as I could, my hands shaking a bit as I opened Mac's dinner can.

Today had freaked me out more than I could

ever let anyone know. That vamp almost had me. I rolled my car. I owed an elf a favor.

I popped the cap on a second beer and walked back into the living room.

Killian was lounging on my fat, plaid couch looking like he was ready to move in.

"Your home is quite pleasant," he said, waving his bottle in the general direction of everywhere.

My place was a cozy two-story, arts and crafts style cottage I had picked up earlier this year. I had some extra cash and needed a change in scenery, so I met up with a nice realtor witch who was able to pluck my dream house straight out of my brain and, with a few tweaks, grow this place for me. It was almost all I had ever hoped for, but to Killian, I just shrugged, "Yah... well. It works."

"You have many human items here, down to this delicious beverage we are partaking of."

"I spend a lot of time on Earth."

The truth be told, I had never quite felt right living in the Other Side.

My father had been an Other Sider, though. He met my mom on Earth. They set up house, had two kids, and for awhile, we lived the California dream. But they had to move the family to the Other Side of the border after a little incident where I discovered I wasn't quite Earth material.

Some guy on the playground made fun of my math skills. So I tried to deck him. He ducked and my hand disappeared. I punched through dimensions. Most cultures would have thrown me a coming of age party, but evidently this Quinceañera involved packing boxes and a moving van.

My sister was smart. She hightailed it back to Earth as soon as she could steal Mom and Dad's keys. Got herself a nice boring little job in finance. But with my special little gifts, I was stuck living amongst the magical folk.

No matter what wonders lay on the Other Side, it wasn't where I grew up and, color me crazy, I kind of liked the order found in a place that abided by the laws of physics.

But a girl has to pay her rent, and since my typing skills were lackluster, I went into the tracking business with my dad. And business is business.

"Okay, Killian. Tell me what I need to know."

Killian put down his drink, "Tracker Maggie, there are terrible things that walk the night..."

"In plain speak, please."

He breathed deep at the difficulty of translation. Ah, elves. Only they would get bent out of shape for having to say things as they actually are.

"We are in trouble and we need your help."

I nodded. Now we were getting somewhere.

"What kind of trouble?"

"There is an imbalance. Echoes from this world are appearing in the other."

"I don't follow."

"That invisible hand that threw your...car..."

I could see he totally wanted to say "moving vehicle" or "mechanical steed" or something equally ridiculous. I wasn't going to make this easy on him.

He shook his head in frustration. "It has been some years since I took Human Dialects 401 at university. I was once fluent," he offered apologetically, "It is why I was sent."

Yes, Human Dialects 401 is an actual upper level class here on the Other Side. It's a requirement for any Other Side language major, so that told me this guy wasn't a slouch. Sure, English wasn't too far off for the elves, but sorting out American sayings from Cockney slang, Chinese euphemisms from Hindi cuss words, well... it takes a pretty smart cookie. I spoke a little Elfish myself, but sounded more like a bad actor in a community theater production of *Julius Caesar*.

"It'll come back to you," I said as I leaned back and took another sip of my beer. "Keep going."

He closed his eyes again in concentration,

"That force that threw your car... It has been happening all along the boundary. My mistress, the Queen of the Elves, wishes to put a stop to it."

Crap.

"The Queen of the Elves wants ME to look into this."

Killian nodded.

"Why me?" I asked, rubbing my forehead, wishing that this was all just a bad fucking dream.

"Your family can walk within the two worlds thanks to your father's powers. Your family can see through the boundary and sometimes into the future thanks to your mother's gift of sight. The Queen has heard you possess both their gifts."

He was right. I did. My specialty was portal creation, though. I could get from Earth to the Other Side with a little more than a howdy do.

That said, I didn't want to howdy anything he was doing.

"Is it too late to back out of that favor?"

Killian took my hand in his, and perhaps it was just the effects of shot-gunning two twelve ounce bottles in five minutes, but I didn't punch him in the nose.

"Dear Maggie, we know the vampire who almost killed you today was no accident. He was not like those you normally track."

I thought back to the words the sucker had

uttered as we had struggled.

"He said there is a bounty on my head..."

Killian nodded. I hated that I knew he wasn't lying.

"Any idea why?"

"My mistress believes it is because you are a child of your particular parents, parents with gifts of dimension travel and sight."

Ah, family.

"So, this makes the bad guys want me dead or alive?"

Killian nodded again, "Or worse."

He got me right where he needed me. Dead I could handle. It's the "or worse" part that sends chills down my bones.

"Crap."

I leaned back against the couch. I was spooked.

"You are not alone in the Queen's task," Killian said.

"We're all alone," I replied.

"I am here on behalf of the elfin kingdom to aid you."

I rose from my seat, "Show yourself out. We'll talk tomorrow."

With that, I walked upstairs and went to bed.

Chapter 6

I woke up with Mac smothering my face. I don't know what it is about cats and the whole "the rest of the bed is not good enough for me, I want to be where your head is" action, but fortunately, he's cute, so I let him live.

The sun was shining through my windows and I stretched to greet the day.

And then remembered the conversation from the night before.

What a way to ruin a perfectly good morning.

Desperate times call for desperate measures and it appeared to be time to pull out the big guns.

Time to visit my mom.

I walked downstairs and realized there was a man sleeping on my couch. Okay, so an elf man, but a figure of the male species. Killian, rather than showing himself out, had decided to spend the night. God, the elfin men are pretty creatures. I tried to ignore the way the sun and shadows lay upon his face, causing his sleepy bed head to glow like an angel's halo. It was nothing but elfin magic and I knew better.

Great.

The day was improving with each passing moment.

I stomped into the kitchen and fired up the coffee pot - Other Side or Earth, there is only one civilized way to greet the day. While it perked, I fed Mac, since it appeared his highness was on the brink of starvation, and set about getting breakfast for us second class citizens. I was slicing the bagels and fruit when I felt Killian's presence even before he spoke.

"That looks good," he said, wrapping his arms around me. "Good morning, partner." He then walked over and helped himself to the coffee, leaving me standing there with a knife in my hand and the unfortunate decision whether or not to disembowel him. Since it was before my first cup, I decided to wait until the caffeine kicked in.

"You're still here," I remarked dryly.

Killian shrugged, "Think of me as your own personal body guard."

"I'm a tracker. I don't need a body guard."

"Then why did you sleep with your neck guard on?"

My hand reached up and touched the Kevlar collar. In truth, I had been so tired, I had just forgotten. Or at least, I wanted to tell myself that was the only reason. I had learned to fall asleep in it long ago. The sun was up, though, and there wasn't any need for it during the day.

"I just forgot."

I twirled the dial of the locks, my fingers knowing the clicks to release the combination. It opened slowly like a heavy door. I took it off and placed it on the counter, rubbing where it had cut into my skin overnight.

I could see Killian's eyes widen as he looked at my neck. I had gotten used to that look. Hellz, you'd think a guy had never seen a girl with scars before. I had plenty more to shock him with.

It was just that the scars were on my neck. A vamp gets your carotid artery and you're done. He'll either kill you or turn you and there's no going back. One of those bastards almost got me. Once. I staked him good and enjoyed the sound of puncturing his heart. Still, he left me with a mess of scars that no amount of makeup could cover and nightmares that still left me drenched in sweat. That's when I started wearing the neckguard. It helped.

Killian raised his hand as if to touch one. I involuntarily flinched away.

"Don't."

"What happened?"

"You'll have to buy me a couple more drinks

before you get that story out of me."

He lowered his hand and nodded, before volunteering, "I could make them go…"

I cut him off. I knew what he was trying to say, "What, and owe you another favor? Not on your life." I pulled two dishes out of the yellow cupboard and made up breakfast plates for both of us, "Besides, they're from a vamp. There's nothing anyone can do."

Killian stepped back, "My apologies."

I had accepted the horror of them long ago, "Yah, well, they cut short my burgeoning career as a supermodel…"

We both sat silently, lost in thought as we ate our breakfast.

"I think they make you look even lovelier," Killian finally said quietly. "Please pass the bagels."

I suddenly felt very awkward. So I lobbed the bagel at his head.

Chapter 7

Elves are not fans of driving. Shoot, they could run faster than I could drive, especially in Other Side traffic, but Killian was buckled up in my passenger seat, ready to start our grand adventure ridding the world from the forces of evil, before I could shoo him away.

I had other plans.

"Listen, Killian, I appreciate the whole protection thing and stuff, but I've got an errand I need to run."

"I shall go with you."

"The kind of errand that I need you not to go on with me."

If it is of a personal nature, have no fear of offending me..."

Part of me thought about bringing him along just to see him suffer, but then the little angel on my shoulder started whispering about the fact he staked a vampire for me and I probably owed him.

"I have to go see my mother, all right?"

Yah, that made the blood drain from his face.

"You may let me off at the mouth to the Woods," he said.

Smart man. I wished I could go with him.

I pulled over in front of the arched gate, its carved wooden flourishes marking the entrance to the elves' domain. I waved to the horse and cart behind me to go around. The horse gave me a disgusted glare as he passed, his owner gave me a sympathetic nod.

"Okay, Killian. Here you go."

"I shall await your return."

God, the guy just doesn't get a hint.

"Listen, Killian, you're really nice, but you're walking that fine line between clingy and stalker-esque. I promise I will make good on that favor owed, but you gotta give me a little space."

"I am here to help."

Without thinking, I accidentally looked deep into those baby blues of his and man, I was going to have to turn on the defroster to unfog the windows. I couldn't seem to get my mouth and my brain to synchronize.

I closed my eyes, "Turn off the glamour, punk. I fight the bad guys, right? I can't be getting all mushy if there is ass kicking to do."

"I apologize. I forget my effect on human women."

Right. How convenient.

But the pheromone ocean subsided and my pulse slowed down to a normal enough rate to hear him when he said, "Maggie, after you speak with your mother, please do not go after this foe alone."

That made me look at him a second time, "Wait. What does this have to do with my mom?"

"My Queen has directed that I say no more."

I suddenly felt like I was about to learn that I had walked into a great big game show of The Multiverse's Next Top Stooge, "Riiiight."

Killian exited my car and leaned against the doorframe for a moment to let me know, "I shall wait for you here."

I put the car into gear and drove off wondering, as I stared at him in my rear view mirror, what he wasn't telling me.

Chapter 8

The neon palmist sign hummed in the red curtained window, foxglove and wolfsbane growing in the postage stamp sized yard. I opened up the picket gate and walked down the cobblestones to the front door.

"Hey, Maggie! Long time, no see!"

I waved at my mom's neighbor, Jack. He owned the business next door. He was a fix-it man, a jack-of-all-trades. Get it? Ba-d-um-dum-ching. Oh, the Other Siders and their highbrow humor.

This was an older part of town, filled with curiosity shops and bakeries. Mom owned a psychic eye tearoom/den and ran it out of the front of her house. Psychic shops were about as glamorous in the Other Side as Radio Shacks are on Earth, but Mom had a dedicated clientele and had proven time and again that she had the gift.

Which is why I didn't visit very much.

"MAGGIE!!! Who is the tall blonde man?"

Christ. Already...

Mom stepped through the beaded curtain separating the living room from the kitchen. She wore a purple muumuu, her curly red hair fro'ed out in a triangle around her head.

"Hey Mom..."

She gathered me up in her arms and gave me a sound kiss on the cheek, "You need to visit more often. I know you won't be back for a couple weeks, but still, you should stop by."

"I'll try. Things have been very busy lately..."

"Sit down! Sit down! I have your favorite tea brewing!"

I sat on the poufy couch, sinking in between the tasseled pillows and feeling like I was twelve years old again.

"You're lucky that vampire didn't get you last night!" she called from the other room.

"I was wearing protection!"

She hustled back in with two steaming cups on saucers, "Well, you woke me in the middle of the night. I thought I was going to have a heart attack. A mother shouldn't have to feel that much fear coming from her daughter. Can't you find a nice daytime job? Perhaps something in cosmetics?"

This was not going well. I went to sip the tea, but she stopped me, "Don't scald your tongue."

I stopped and blew upon the surface dutifully.

"Now, tell me about this tall blonde man in your life." She practically bounced as she asked.

"He's an elf..."

"Ooo. Do tell! I've always loved the elves."

"I know, Mom," I said, trying hard not to die.

"So, he is an elf..."

"Yes, he's an elf named Killian..."

"And he mysteriously came into your life..."

I set down my teacup, "Do you want me to tell you or do you want to save me some time?"

She gave me a wink and pushed my teacup towards my mouth like a toddler who can't figure out his sippy cup, "Drink up, dear, drink up!"

"Mom, he said that there is a break in the border between the Other Side and Earth. He said I'm the only one who can stop this. He said you'd know why."

Well, that shut her up.

I've never seen my mom scared.

I mean, she pulled the injured bird act whenever she needed to manipulate a situation in her favor, but my mom is a force of nature. So, I was a little thrown when her teacup started rattling in her hand. She sank into her chair and put her drink on the table beside her, "I did not see this coming."

That was a first.

"See what, Mom?"

She jumped up and began pacing the room, wringing her hands, "I thought we had left this all behind us."

"What are you talking about?"

"Of course you wouldn't know..."

"Mom?"

"I should have told you sooner..."

"MOM?"

"How was I to know that he would find us here..."

"MOTHER WHAT ARE YOU TALKING ABOUT?"

"Your uncle, dear."

The words knocked me flat on my ass. I had no uncle.

"What?'

Mom came over and patted me on the knee, "Your uncle. We thought this chapter of our life was over, so that's why your father and I never spoke with you about it."

"We have an uncle?"

It was a foreign word on my tongue. Uncle. Family. Beyond my parents and my sister. I had an extended family. I mean, sure it was too late for him to take me to the zoo and buy me a camel ride, but still. I had an uncle.

"He wasn't a very nice man," she said.

Strike that, I had an evil uncle.

"Whose brother?" I asked.

"Your father's, dear."

And then Mom let out a deep sigh and her face became very serious. She tucked a loose strand of my dark hair behind my ear, "Did you ever wonder why we moved to the Other Side?"

I had. I had wondered every day since I was ten years old and had come home to find all of our belongings in a moving truck. I had wondered as we had made that drive up Mulholland and driven off the cliff. I had wondered as we dropped into the Other Side with its steam powered machines and nightmarish creatures. I had wondered every day as I tucked garlic cloves in my pockets and strapped a crossbow across my back. The Other Side is no place for a human child to grow up.

"You said it was because I was beginning to show that we were not like other families."

"That was a half truth, Maggie. I'm afraid it was more because your uncle was beginning to realize that we were not like other families."

"I don't understand."

"When I met your father, I was reading cards on a folding table down in Santa Monica. He saw me and I saw him and we knew that we were meant for one another. But he was an Other Sider and I was a human – a gifted human, but a human, nonetheless. Your father's brother felt like this was... inappropriate... for your dad to mix with someone like me. Your uncle, his name is Ulrich..."

"Wait, I have an Uncle Ulrich?"

"It does have a rather nice ring, doesn't it?"

"No, I was about to say..." I don't know. Creepy. Unnerving. The perfect name for a criminal overlord? "Never mind..."

"Well, dear, he decided to take it upon himself to discourage our marriage. We hid there on Earth for as long as we could, but when your gifts started coming to light, we couldn't hide amongst normal mortals any longer. The good news was that your uncle didn't have the powers your father did to travel back and forth over the border. Ulrich made it to Earth, but he couldn't make it back to the Other Side. So we came here and we made sure he stayed there."

The lights sorta started coming on in my head.

My official condition was classified as "World Walker" in the Other Side Journal of Medical Magic. It is a pretty elite club. My dad was amazing. He could go back and forth between dimensions like most folks walk between rooms. I'm good but no one, living or dead or undead, has ever held a candle to my dad's skills.

Over the years, the world walkers have created the permanent portals that made it possible for day-trippers to go take a look around Earth and get back. The official portals are carefully monitored and tracked. But there is a booming business of folks who try to predict where the veil is going to be randomly thin and queue up those who might welcome an under-the-radar opportunity to pop on through.

The problem with those naturally occurring portals is that while you can get over to Earth fairly easily, returning to the Other Side is a bitch. You have to reopen the portal, but there is very little magic on Earth. You have to be pretty frickin' powerful to bend the physical laws enough to let you through.

That, too, was why my dad was so special. And why his disappearance had come as such a shock. He was helping me with a run. I came home okay. He didn't. I went back and looked for him. His signature said he stepped through the door, he just never reemerged. It happens. When someone is too weak, the portal will collapse, killing them instantly, or at least we all hope that they are killed instantly. I just didn't think that day would be the last time I'd hear him laugh or call me Maggie-girl.

"So, Uncle Ulrich is trying to come home..." I said.

"I would assume so."

"By destroying the border and bringing down

all of civilization with it?"

Mom sighed, "Like I said, he wasn't a very nice man. Not like your father."

Now it was my turn to pace. I picked up my now lukewarm tea and chugged it. I flipped it upside-down on the cup, "Read them."

Mom held up her hands, "Now dear, you know I can't do that when you are so angry..."

"READ THEM."

Mom took the saucer out of my hand and lifted the cup. She stared at the leaves and sighed, "It's him. And he's tearing down the boundary. And you need to leave for Los Angeles tonight. Well, that's good to know I won't see you for a couple weeks because you're out of town, not that you hate me."

"I don't hate you, Mother."

"A child will never fully understand a mother's love."

I could feel a headache coming on, "Just keep reading."

"Well, that's just about it."

"No, is there anything about what I should do when I get there? How I find him? How I can cause him to stop?"

"No. But it does say you should bring that gorgeous elf you've been traveling with."

"Is that really true or do you just want me to

have a guy around?"

"Dating never hurt anyone, dear..."

"Mom..." I warned.

"Honey, I'm not getting any younger and I would like to be able to enjoy my time with my grandchildren."

"Mom. I'm here asking you about keeping our two worlds from colliding and keeping the physical space of the universe intact and you're concerned about my love life?"

"I just think you might be missing out on some of life's greatest pleasures."

"I'm fine. Just... read. Read the tea leaves."

She put down the saucer, "They don't say anything else."

"Now, don't pout."

"I'm not pouting."

"Mom, the information you have might be vital. Tell me what to do?"

She got up and wandered back to the kitchen. I could hear her washing the dish in the sink. "You never listen to me anyways," she called.

"I'm listening!"

She stood in the doorway, "They don't say anything else that I can tell you. Just go to Los Angeles. Bring Killian. And don't die."

"Two out of three?" I offered, thinking it would be so much easier to leave Killian in the forest.

"All of them, honey."

"Will I be successful?"

"Would I be standing here fighting with you if I thought you were even capable of failing?" She came over and wrapped me up in her arms, "Your father would be proud."

Mom was soft. I leaned up against her. All I could think was that I still missed Dad so much it hurt.

She kissed me on my temple, "Me, too, dear."

Chapter 9

I blasted the A/C the moment I started the car. Double rising suns make for some gnarly car bake. I cranked up my radio and tried to drown out the voices in my head with some old skool Guns 'n Roses. But "Sweet Child of Mine" just made me think about my dad, which made me think about my mom, which brought me back to the fact I had an evil uncle who was tearing down the boundary between two planes of existence and the entire fate of several worlds was somehow now my responsibility.

Crap.

My cell phone chirped and I picked it up. No, Verizon doesn't cover the Other Side with its 4G network. We have our own version of contract mobile hell to deal with.

"Maggie speaking," I barked into the receiver.

"Maggie, we have another skip. Ghoul seems to have decided to go day tripping. You in?" asked Lacy.

"I'll swing by to pick up the paperwork now."

Nothing got my spirits soaring like work and nothing sent them stratospherically like something to distract me from a bigger problem.

I pulled into the courthouse, a gothic nightmare of grey stones and cold iron. Guess they wanted all the bureaucrats to feel at home. The guards on the turrets lowered their crossbows as they saw who it was. I gave them a little wave as I drove across the drawbridge.

I parked right next to the Bureau of Records and jumped out of my car.

The office was cramped. Filing cabinets and a large desk took up most of the space. What was left over was taken up by the ogre processing paperwork.

"Hey, Frank!"

He looked up at me with his one eye and sighed, "Shit. You? They had to call you?"

"Easy, Frank, you'll make me think you don't like me."

He let out a huff, sending a rank breeze of halitosis my way. Eyes watering, I reached into my bag and pulled out a box, "Breath mint?"

"You're lucky I let you live." He took a mint in his massive paws and chewed it thoughtfully before handing me a folder, "Here's the skip. Ghoul named Izpanki. Said he had business on the

41

Other Side and outstayed his travel plans."

I flipped through the file. Seemed routine enough. Ghouls are tough in that they can take the form of whatever they have most recently eaten, but are notoriously lazy and tend to hang out in cemeteries like nursing home residents waiting for the buffet line to open.

I tucked the file in my purse, "Thanks, Frank. I will count the moments until we are reunited."

Frank let out a loud, ripping fart and then smirked at me.

I seriously needed to reconsider my career path.

As I drove away, I began to mentally note all the items needing to be checked off prior to departure. Laundry, cat sitter for Mac...

...and Killian.

He said he would be waiting for me, and as I turned the corner, sure enough, there he was, perched on one leg like a goddamned stork. Knowing he'd stand like that for a century without shifting, I decided I should relieve the poor bastard.

I pulled in front of him and opened the door from the inside. He hopped in and buckled his seatbelt, "Did you learn anything of use?"

"Yah."

"Care to expound?"

I sighed, "Mom said my uncle is responsible

for the weakening border. He got stuck on Earth and is probably trying to get home to the Other Side. She said I should bring you with me."

"I have always thought her to be a wise woman."

"You know my mom?"

"Know 'of' your mom."

"Let's keep it that way, shall we?"

I pulled into the driveway of my home, shut off the car and gathered up my files.

"What is that in your hand?" Killian asked, pointing at the file about the ghoul.

"Eh, just a job I decided to pick up."

He placed his hand on my arm, "I am sorry if I was not clear, but you have a task you are bound to."

"Don't get your boxers in a bunch. I may be bound to save the world, but I have bills."

"My mistress, the Queen of the Elves, can provide for you..."

I held up my hand and stopped him right there, "Listen, it's bad enough I have to haul you around, I'm not going on any magical princess's payroll. Besides, it gives us a great cover while we hunt down my uncle. Now, would you get out of my way so I can open the door?"

Once inside, I placed a couple calls, begged a professional service to make sure nothing ate

Mac while I was gone, and went upstairs to throw some clothes into my suitcase. But as soon as I shut the bedroom door behind me, I picked up the phone again.

"Hello?" came a soft, feminine voice on the other end.

"Mindy!"

"Maggie?"

Mindy was that twin sister of mine living on Earth - married to a really nice guy named Austin, two car household, family dog, flossed regularly and ate five fruits and vegetables a day.

I tucked the phone on my shoulder and started packing. I could hear pots and pans clanging in the background. I'm sure she was probably whipping together a caramelized duck l'orange soufflé casserole flambé from scratch or something.

"Mind if I come hang out in your guest room for a week or so?"

"Why...?" she asked cautiously.

It should tell you a lot about our relationship that she knew enough to ask "why".

"Listen, there is something happening... actually, I can't talk about it on the phone. Can I come?"

"Of course," she said. And that was why she was the best sister. Whether it meant her neck was at risk or not, the door was always open.

"Oh… and do you mind if I bring a guest with me?"

"Who?"

"A guy I know…"

"MAGGIE!!! We've been on the phone all this time and you didn't tell me about a guy? Are you coming across to tell us you've met someone?"

I couldn't even stifle the laugh, "No."

I could almost hear her wilt with disappointment over the phone.

"Well, fine. But you better be at least sleeping with him."

"I'll see you tonight, okay?"

"Okay. I love you."

"Love you, too."

And with that, we hung up in complete sync.

My house was one of the few houses in the Other Side with a direct line to Earth. It was a slight misuse of power, but whatevs. Just one of those little perks of Dad's gift.

I threw my duffel bag to the bottom of the steps. There was nothing in it that would break.

I entered the room. Killian was sitting with his leg up in my armchair, all tunic and tights.

"So, do we need to swing by your place to pick up some stuff?" I asked him.

"I am ready whenever you are, sweet Maggie."

45

I eyed up his gold threaded doublet and poofy sleeves. Great. He was going to blend in like a circus clown at the New York Stock Exchange. But, hellz, if he wanted to go running around Earth looking like he had escaped duties at the RenFest, who was I to judge.

"Come give me a hand," I sighed.

He followed me into my spare room. In the corner stood my dusty computer and an unused futon. I opened up the closet and flipped open a console hidden behind a sliding panel. I input a sequence of letters and numbers, and the wall opened up to reveal my armory. Killian gave a low whistle.

"What? You've never seen a girl's hope chest before?" I said.

He smiled and chuckled, "I am afraid you are not quite like the other girls I have known, Maggie."

I pulled down my crossbow with the silver tipped bolts, my Remington Model 870 shotgun, my Bushmaster AR-15 Semiautomatic Rifle, my Smith & Wesson Model 10 Revolver, my Colt M1911, my Glock 22, several flasks of St. Ubaldus's Highly Holy Water, a couple crucifixes blessed at Lourdes, my Tiffany silver stakes, a MLB approved Pro Stock Louisville Slugger, and a basket full of organic garlic heads from a Whole Witch Natural Food Markets. Killian's eyes widened.

"You gonna give me a hand carrying this all out to the car or what?" I asked.

He dutifully picked up the bags as I packed them and began hauling.

I looked out the window. The sun was starting to set. It had been a full day. I walked into the kitchen where I had taken off my neckguard and clicked it back into place, spinning the dials of the locks as Killian re-entered.

"We should get moving before dark," I said. "Things that go bump in the night and all."

He nodded.

I poured a couple bowls of dry cat food for Mac and filled up his water fountain. Yes, my cat has one of those fountains from the Sky Mall. I might spend my day killing monsters with icy cold focus, but I wasn't heartless. You think about drinking out of a stale cup all day. I let Killian and myself out, locking the door behind me.

Dusk was just starting to settle across the landscape.

As were several dark shapes flying over the treetops.

"Shit shit shit shit shit. Killian? We have company! Get in the car!"

He looked up and took off at a full sprint. We hit the car at the same time and had the doors open, shut, locked, and car revved before the vamps hit my property line.

"Bounty on my head, huh?"

Killian nodded as he tried to see where they went.

That's when I heard the thud on the roof of my car as the first vamp landed. His nails punctured through the metal like knives through rice paper.

"Fuck. Now I'm going to have to use an umbrella in the car when it rains."

I cornered hard and could hear him sliding. His feet dangled by Killian's window. He got in a good kick and a circular spider web fractured the glass.

"Do me a favor. Reach out your window and yank him off, would you?"

"The glass will not roll down..." Killian said, frantically pressing the window button.

P.O.S. car. I cornered hard to the right. The vampire slid the other way. I rolled down my window to keep from having to make another call to my insurance company.

"Take the wheel."

Foot heavy on the gas as Killian steered, I reached out with two hands and yanked the vamp hard. I could feel his cold muscles struggle to climb back onto the roof.

"Turn right! Turn right!" I shouted at Killian.

The momentum of the car flung the vamp and

I could hear his torso hit the roof hard as his legs flew out. I reached into the top of my boot and pulled out my silver spike. I slammed it through the roof as Killian continued to corner the car. I heard an inhuman scream. The nails retracted from the roof. I rolled up the window and pulled out the spike. I saw the vampire fall off the car and onto the road. Two more vampires dropped out of the sky to check in on him.

Unfortunately, Killian was still cornering and I got a great big eye lock with 'em before I could wrest the wheel away. Locking eyes with a vampire: "Way To Get Yourself Killed Right Quick #84" in the *Idiots Guide to Not Getting Dead By A Monster*. I could hear their siren call of seduction and felt a none too unpleasant sensation down in the general direction of my hoohaw.

"Maggie, stay with me!"

And then I felt a stinging slap across my face as well as a healthy whiff of leather and man.

I looked at Killian, his hands still on the wheel.

"You back?" he asked.

"Yah. Thanks."

I grabbed the wheel from him and gunned my car straight at the vamps. I hit them like a pair of ten pins in a macabre game of Bowling for Blood. The vamp on the ground and a second guy went under my wheels. The third hit my hood and then went over the top of my car. I looked into my rear view.

Yah, it's only on Earth that you can't see them in a mirror.

I glanced over at Killian. His pupils were dilated as he hung onto the suicide handle.

The grin crept to the corners of my mouth and spread into a wide smile. "That was hot," I said.

Killian shook his head and laughed, "You, my dear Maggie, are sick."

Chapter 10

Earth seemed so quiet compared to the Other Side. I slowed down as we cruised over Barham, past the movie studios in Burbank, and headed out the 134 freeway towards Pasadena. Once you get past Glendale, civilization falls away and the freeway cuts through the rolling hills like a bird. You feel almost like you're flying above the glittering homes tucked into the valleys below. This time of night, the road was empty and there was nothing but the distant sprawl of the city and the stars.

I rolled down my one working window and smelled the dusty sage in the air. This was home – driving through the hills at night in this crazy, messed up world of false dreams.

Killian cleared his throat, "You did an excellent job defending us."

I glanced at him outta the side of my lids, realizing he was trying to pay me a compliment.

"You didn't do so badly yourself," I offered with about as much grace as a kindergartener on the playground. "Thanks for giving me a smack when that bastard caught my eyes."

"My pleasure," he replied. A silence hung between us for a moment. "I have wanted to do that since the moment I met you."

I laughed, "The feeling's mutual."

He held out his hand, "Partners?"

"Yah," I said, as I took my hand off the wheel and shook on it, "Partners."

He smiled, "So, where are you taking me, partner?"

"My sister's place."

"Sister?"

"Twin sister."

"I did not know that you had family on Earth."

"Yah. The super human powers and ability to jump reality lines were all eaten up by my embryo. Mindy's a run-of-the-mill human. The Other Side can be deadly for her type."

I exited the freeway and drove down the tree-lined street to a well-kept Victorian home with a tidy garden and ancient trees. I pulled up the driveway and parked in front of the garage.

Killian had picked up all of the bags before I could even ask him for help. I gave him a grin and practically ran up the stairs to the porch. I knocked on the wooden screen door and heard footsteps come closer.

It opened up and there was my sister. She squealed like a little girl and jumped up and down, planting a great big kiss on my cheek. Then out came her husband, Austin, and it was a blur of introductions as they shook Killian's hand and eyed up his tunic.

"Nice outfit," Austin remarked.

"I am an elf."

"Got it," Austin punched me in the shoulder with a knowing glance, "Nicely played, Maggie."

"We're just working together," I insisted. "One case. That's it."

Killian draped his arm around my waist, "We are very happy in our new partnership together."

Austin winked at me and motioned for Killian to follow him to the back guest room. Guess they needed some private guy-to-guy time to discuss monster trucks and farting.

Mindy led me upstairs to the room she kept just for me. Her great big Irish setter placed his wet nose in the palm of my hand and danced around in excitement.

My room was covered in pink, cabbage rose wallpaper with shabby chic flair, which was so my sister. The bed was piled high with feather comforters and deep pillows. It was a softness I didn't feel I could justify in my own life, with its harsh edges and realities. But here... here it was like a vacation.

I felt absolutely filthy and started stripping down right then and there, starting with my neck protection. There was nothing to fear here. Mindy had garlic tucked into every dried wreath and every window had a cross worked into the stained glass. She took no chances.

She sat down on the bed and grimaced, "Ick. Just watching you take that off gives me the creeps. I don't know how you can live over there, Maggie."

I laughed as I sat on the window seat and started removing all the knives and pointy things hidden on my person, "I wonder that myself every single frickin' day."

"Guess it can't be too bad with a hunk-a-hunk of burning elf there to ease your sorrows..."

I looked at her, "You realize I'm still armed, right?"

"What?" she asked, batting her eyes. "He's cute."

"He's a fucking elf," I said, tossing a couple throwing stars onto the mirrored dressing table.

"Well, at least I know why I haven't seen you for so long."

"You're starting to sound like Mom," I warned, pointing a stake at her.

"How is she doing?" Mindy asked with such warmth and love. Evidently, absence makes the heart grow forgetful of all the passive aggressive guilt or something.

I sighed, "Crazy as ever. Don't you two talk on the phone, like, every day?"

"But I just wonder how she's doing, for real."

I gave a shrug, "She seems to be holding up well. Barely mentions Dad anymore, so at least she's stopped pretending he's coming back."

Mindy shook her head, "She knew better..."

So, here's the deal. You can't read your own future. Everyone knows that, but Mom decided she was an exception to the rule. For almost three years, she had tried gazing into her own fortune and believing in the signs she thought she was seeing. I wanted Dad magically alive again as bad as anyone. Hell, I was at ground zero when it happened. I spent my share of nights wondering what I could have done differently. But wounds can't heal if you keep them open with false hope. Hope just makes it worse.

Austin came into the room and threw himself on the bed beside Mindy, completely messing up the artfully placed pillows. Mindy gave a sigh.

"Killian's getting settled. How long are you here?" he asked.

"Don't know. Got myself a skip and another gig, so, we'll see."

Mindy snapped her fingers, "Oh! What

was that thing you weren't allowed to talk about?"

Ah jeez, there wasn't going to be any way to pussyfoot around the topic, so I just laid it out for her, "Evidently some nutter is trying to weaken the boundary between Earth and the Other Side."

Mindy sat straight up, "What?"

"And what's worse is that it turns out that nutter is our uncle."

"We don't have an uncle."

"Actually, we do. Dad had an evil brother."

"Nice of Mom and Dad to tell us about this."

I waved my hand dismissively, "Yah, I guess he came over to Earth to kill us all and then, I guess, this is just from Mom's side of things, he got stranded here and now is trying to get back to the Other Side."

"Are you here to take him back over?" asked Mindy.

"Just trying to get him to quit trying to tear through dimensions and stuff. Hopefully, I can stop the guy from destroying the boundary and he can cool his jets here on Earth in a nice little retirement village or something."

Austin looked over at Mindy and gave her hands a squeeze, "I'll make sure to have all our security systems checked in the morning."

"And here you thought you knew what you were getting into when you married me. Surprise," Mindy said as she planted a kiss on his cheek, "Okay, family gossip is officially banned for the next hour while I get dinner ready."

Mindy heaved herself from the bed, "And you, sir, are going to help me peel carrots."

With a pleading look to me, Austin groaned as Mindy pulled him up, "Save me!"

But I'm afraid there are some types of trouble beyond even my powers.

Chapter 11

After dinner, Killian and I sat in the living room as Mindy and Austin cleaned up. Mindy is one of those gals who never lets a guest help. I quit fighting years ago and tonight I was only too happy to surrender to my belly full of dessert and her comfy couch. Killian sat beside me looking positively drunk on the sugar high.

"I like pie."

I patted his knee as he gave me a blissed out little grin. I dunno what my sister put in with the pecans and caramel, but Killian looked like he might be seeing The Face of God. My sister had some mad kitchen skills. I was more the Sara-Lee-thaw-it-on-the-counter type. Sometimes even that was too much work.

Austin came out with cups of coffee and set about firing up the fireplace.

"So if you were my dad's evil brother, where would you hide?" I asked him as he got the kindling going.

Austin shrugged his shoulders as he stepped back from his handy work, "No idea, but I have to say, I'm so disappointed you had an evil uncle and didn't even know it. No trips to his evil lair or sitting by his side as he took over the world. You totally got gypped."

Mindy came out, mug in hand and grinned, "I'm sure as soon as she finds him, Maggie will make up for lost time."

I laughed, "This family reunion is in dangerous peril if I can't even figure out where to start."

"Google him?" offered Austin.

"Right. A Google search. With the key words 'Ulrich MacKay Evil Dimension Destroyer'. I'm sure the hits will just come rolling in."

"Have you checked Dad's office downtown?" asked Mindy. "Maybe some of his old co-workers know something."

This was news to me. I looked over at her, "I helped Dad all the time. When was he working downtown?"

Mindy blinked, "I always figured the two of you were over at his office filing for justice or billing the forces of evil."

I shook my head, "Never seemed to be 'Bring Your Daughter to Work Day'." I looked at Killian and shrugged, "Maybe it's time to see if there is some family business I should be taking over."

Chapter 12

Mindy had a phone number. Evidently, Dad had given it to her in case of emergency. I figured this qualified. I did a reverse trace and found an address.

The roads of downtown LA are a bizarre mash-up of good times gone by and really good times gone by. Homeless crackheads camp out beneath the art deco marquees of some of the most beautiful theaters ever to be abandoned. Sure, much of the space had been converted to lofts and fancy living, but the folks in those homes lived like robber barons under siege, locked behind iron worked gates and security codes. They were posh overlords with a panoramic view of skid row from every floor-to-ceiling window.

I don't know if the darkening light was from the shadows of the high rises or something more sinister, but when we turned off Maple into the Toy District, a rundown block of wholesale electronics and piñatas, my Creeped-Out-O-Meter was in the red zone.

I pulled the car over and parked, inserted something crazy like seven dollars worth of quarters into the meter for a measly hour, and we walked down the alley.

There were twinkle lights and faint guitar music drifting down the way. We stopped in front of a small café whose sign read, "El Diablo."

I looked over at Killian, "Can you think of any scenario in which this ends well?"

"No."

I sighed, "Let's go."

We climbed the stairs and entered the shop. It was huge inside with voodoo masks hanging turquoise walls. A tattooed man tended the coffee bar while a guy with a scraggly beard strummed the song we had been hearing.

"Other Siders out back," said the inked dude.

"Excuse me?" I said.

"You heard me. No elves in the front."

Killian and I looked at each other and then walked into the back room. It was a covered patio with tables and heat lamps. An empty bar sat to the side beneath the metal roofing. The tables and chairs were mismatched wood. They all looked like they had been there for a long time.

Sitting at one of the tables was a fat man in a shiny grey suit smoking a cigar. His eyes were locked upon us from the time we walked through the door.

"Guess the 'no smoking' ordinance didn't hit this side of town, huh?" I said.

"Does it bother you, little lady?" the fat man leered.

"I'm good," I replied.

"What can I do for you?"

"I don't know. What can you?"

"You have a smart mouth."

Killian placed his hand on my arm, "We are having trouble getting back home."

The fat man leaned back in his seat and laughed, "Other Siders in need a portal? Well, even if I could get you one, it will cost you. How much money do you have?"

"Enough."

"We heard there was a man named Ulrich..." I said. From the look on his face, I immediately realized that I had pretty much sent up a flare signal that we were "not cool".

"How do you know Ulrich?" the fat man asked sharply.

"He's a family friend," I lied.

"He seems to have many family friends."

I gave a shrug.

"I know him," said the fat man. "Let me see if he is around."

He took out his cell phone and typed

something quickly before slowly putting it back in his coat pocket.

The door to the kitchen burst open and four dudes the size of rhinoceroses stormed in.

Seriously, I had no beef with the fat man and there was no need to go bringing a gun to a knife fight. But it was his call.

Killian pulled a collapsible staff out of his sleeve. At least I hope it was up his sleeve, because in his outfit, there were very few other places it could have come from. His staff was the kind you could whack people with one moment and flip into nunchuks the next. He seemed to have his two attackers covered, so I figured I'd take the other two.

The fat man just sat there and watched. Asshole.

"Four against two? Come on," I said.

"I suppose I could make it five, but then it would not be sporting."

A chair came sailing by my head, missing me by inches and clocking the other bad dude who was trying to sneak up behind me in the face. I followed through with a one-two punch to his jaw and in a matter of seconds he was on the ground with little tweetie birds circling.

"You okay, Killian?"

"Managing fairly well..."

He looked like he might be breaking a sweat,

so since I was done with the one guy, I had enough time to strategically land a Doc Marten in a kneecap of another.

The bad guy crumpled with a cry and Killian finished him off with a foot to the nose.

"Maggie!" Killian cried, rolling over my back beer barrel polka style to nail Thing Three, who was coming at me with a sharp pointy object.

"Come on, fat man. We're not trying to permanently hurt anyone here. It's just a conversation until someone loses an eye," I said as I sparred with my attacker, who wasn't going down as easily as the other guys.

"Perhaps if you talked less, you would not be having your current troubles."

"Perhaps if you just told us where Ulrich MacKay was, I would buy you a beer and we could call it a day."

"I am afraid anyone who knows the name of Ulrich is not someone I would be breaking a fast with."

"Breaking a fast... hold on." Nobody talks all old skool without a reason. "Are you a fucking elf?"

"It is amazing what modern day plastic surgery on Earth is capable of, is it not? The doctor took just a little off the top," the fat man said as he showed off his rounded ears.

"Did you notice," *punch* "that I," *roundhouse* "am working with an elf?" a *jab to a left cross.*

Total knock out.

Killian sat down to catch his breath as I took on our final opponent.

"You could help," I said as the guy caught a glancing blow across my chin that could have rung my bell if my dancing skills weren't so sharp.

"We must win honorably, man-to-man, without stooping to the tactics of our enemy. I am going to procure a water." He walked through the door and pointed a finger at the fat man. "Anything?"

"I am without need."

And that fucking fairy walked out to go buy some water from the fucking barista.

"Are you fucking kidding me?"

Killian was back, "I shall leave yours on the table over here."

I landed the final earth shattering blow and stepped over the guy's body to grab the water angrily, "Really?"

Killian placed a calming hand upon my forearm, "Really." He looked at the fat man, "You have seen that we fought fairly without deceit. The rules of engagement would dictate you owe us each a bounty."

Point for the elf. I didn't know there was a random set of secret rules that could win us some favors.

"Indeed. You have bested my champions," the fat man replied, as the inked dude brought him a dainty cup of tea. Of course he would be a fucking tea drinker.

I wasn't any good with setting contracts with fairy folk, so I turned to my partner, "Killian, ask him for something."

Killian pulled out a piece of paper, wrote down my number, and handed it to the fat man, "You are hereby bound to call us immediately with any news of Ulrich MacKay or his whereabouts until the time we deem it fit to cease."

Killian was good.

The fat man nodded his head in acquiescence, "Ulrich has unbalanced the power here. His trade runs have cut into my territory. I would be pleased to assist in... dissuading him... from his current business plan."

I pushed Killian out of the way, "The only dissuading is going to be me punching you in the face. Why did you tell your goons to attack us if we're on the same side?!? Friend of my enemy and all!"

"You did not say that you were friends with my enemy," the fat guy unhelpfully pointed out.

"I didn't know that he wasn't a friend of yours," I countered.

"Then this was nothing more than an unfortunate misunderstanding."

"Listen," I said. "My dad used to spend a bunch of time here, jerkface…"

The fat guy looked at me sharply, "Your father?"

"William MacKay."

"Why did you not say that you were William MacKay's daughter?" he said, all tension gushing out of the room like rioters pouring out of a soccer game.

"Maybe because you sicced four guards on us before we had a chance."

"When the name Ulrich MacKay is mentioned, I have found it is best to make the first move and sort things out later, if there are things to sort out."

"Well… let's… sort some things out," I offered weakly.

"Please, sit," he said, motioning to some chairs.

Killian and I grabbed our bottles and I flung myself into one like a 13-year old girl about to be told she couldn't go to the mall. One of the guards started to stir, so I offered him my hand.

"Your boss has a sick sense of humor," I said, helping him to his feet and brushing the dirt off his tweed suit jacket.

I took a long drag off of my water and then fixed the fat man in my gaze, "Okay. Tell me how you knew my father."

"Your father aided me by transporting sensitive artifacts to private collectors between worlds. He was an 'independent contractor' of sorts."

"My father was a tracker," I corrected.

"No," said the fat man chewing on the soggy end of his cigar, "your father was a smuggler."

"You're a liar," I said.

"Believe or do not believe, it matters not to me. But it is the truth."

"I was with him on every run for the past ten years," I said, leaning forward.

"The antiquities were small baubles - trifles, really. They would not have been noticed."

"Really? And what were these tiny treasures exactly?"

"Vampire relics."

That, I have to say, knocked me on my ass.

"Vampire relics. My dad worked in vampire relics?"

The fat man's eyes were beady and glinted with greasy greed, "You would not happen to be here today to follow in your father's footsteps?"

I gritted my teeth and managed to spit out sweetly, "I'm afraid my current contractual obligations have me all tied up at the moment."

"Tis a pity," said the fat man. "Well, if it

soothes your delicate sensibilities, your father would not take any of my larger jobs - only the vampire relics. In fact, he was the one that contacted me. A very wealthy private collector had asked him to keep his head up. Anything I was able to get my hands on, he was interested in. Of course you know taking relics to the Other Side weakens the vampires' strength here on Earth, which was a win for me. Profit and peace, all wrapped up in a tidy bundle tied with a 24 karat string."

So that's why the vampires were after me. The pieces were starting to fall into place. It was because of this jerk and a burgeoning bank account that I'm sure was as cushy as he.

"Any idea what you stole that might have gotten them worked up?" I asked icily.

"No idea, but if I hear of anything," he waved the little piece of paper with my phone number on it, "I shall give you a ring."

I had had it up to my neckguarded chin, "YOU'RE THE REASON THE ENTIRE VAMPIRE RACE IS TRYING TO KILL ME AND YOU'LL GIVE ME A CALL???"

The fat guy held up his palms in apology, "It is a hazard of my trade. Your father was a valuable asset in my operation, though, and I do not wish for us to part enemies. Your uncle's name always seemed to come up when... how shall I say... a 'trade'... had gone sour. I am not the forgiving type and it would please me to be able to assist you in tracking him down... for justice."

"Well, maybe I'm not the forgiving type either and I don't want to work with the guy who has brought the whole world crashing around my ears," I pointed out.

"Quite understandable. But perhaps you will allow me to secure you a brownie from our bakery in apology."

"Does it have nuts?" I shouted, "Because that's what you are to think that I can be bought off with chocolaty goodness!"

Killian's face cringed.

"What?"

"He did not mean that kind of brownie."

"What???" Then realization dawned and I felt like an ass. "Oh. A brownie."

"Cleaners. Cooks. Ears to the ground," said the fat man.

"Oh. That's different," I said. "That would be... acceptable. And I will take a regular cake-like brownie, too."

Killian collapsed his head in his hand.

"I'm hungry."

And that was that.

I let Killian drive as I nommed the brownie. I

also tried not to pay much attention to the merry little, one-foot tall man with pointy shoes buckled into the back middle seat. His hands were folded happily on his belly and he looked like he had never been so content as to sit in the back of a busted Honda Civic.

I couldn't take it.

"I'm sorry, what was your name?"

"Pipistrelle!"

The brownie's voice sounded like a cartoon character rolling on speed.

"Would you like some of my... chocolate cake square...?"

His eyes lit up like Christmas, "Many thanks!"

He took the half I offered him, which was the size of his head and chewed it slowly, eyes rolling back in ecstasy.

I wiped my hands on my jeans.

"So, Killian, let's review what we learned today. My dad was a vampire relic smuggler. My Uncle Ulrich is currently IN the smuggling business. The vampires want me dead because something was stolen that shouldn't have been stolen. And we are also responsible for a small man that should probably be buckled into a car seat."

"It is farther along the path than we were yesterday."

"I can help!" the brownie in the back piped

up. I turned around. He had a big chocolate mustache from one ear to the next.

I pulled out a Kleenex and passed it back, "You've got a little something on your cheek."

Pipistrelle wiped his face and wadded up the tissue, "I could find your Uncle Ulrich for you!"

We were sort of at a dead end, so I gave a shrug, "Sure. You do that."

The brownie started unbuckling his seatbelt.

"Wait! Pipistrelle, wait! You don't have to go now."

He climbed up on the co-pilot console and patted my shoulder, "It is my pleasure."

His fat little hand moved towards the door handle.

"WAIT! Killian, pull over the car. Pipistrelle, we are stopping the car. Don't get out until the car... PIPISTRELLE!"

I saw his little body tumble out the side into the gutter. Killian pulled the car to a screeching halt. I hopped out the door to see if the poor little brain injured Pipistrelle was okay only to see him skipping merrily along, dodging sticks and stray leaves.

"Pipistrelle! Are you all right?" I shouted after him.

He gave me a friendly little salute.

"How will we find you?"

"I shall find you!" he squeaked before running into a hedge and was gone.

I climbed back into the car, "And here I was going to get him to do my laundry tonight. Well," I popped open my glove compartment and pulled out a manila folder. "Guess while he does our reconnaissance work, we could round up the ghoul and keep my cover intact."

Killian sighed and took the folder from me, knowing he didn't have much room to maneuver on this matter. He flipped through the sheets in between reading street signs, "A ghoul. How do you propose tracking him when he can take on any shape?"

"Ghouls are going to look for the easiest nosh they can find, which, according to the deeply scientific studies of MacKay and MacKay, usually means a funeral," I said in my best second grade teacher voice.

Killian looked at me like I was the insensitive clod that I actually was, "We are going to start crashing funerals?"

"Yep."

Killian looked at the folder, "Maybe we can just stick with tracking down your uncle."

"It'll be fun. A little garlic necklace for you. A little magic rod for me." I looked at him sharply, "Don't say it."

He shut his mouth with a snap and a grin.

We sat in the car in silence.

"I have a magic rod."

"Shut it!"

"I could consider it as payment of the favor you owe me," he offered.

"Don't!" I said, holding up my finger in warning.

"Although, you probably would end up owing me at the end. We could keep track."

"Elf!"

He held up his hands in acquiescence, "There is no need for favors to be an unpleasant experience."

"Listen, you. You had your chance to name your favor and you chose saving the world instead of saving the world in your pants. Next time, bargain better."

He gave me a wink, "That I shall, that I shall…"

Chapter 13

So, Killian wasn't completely off. Ghouls can be darn tricky to spot. That is, they are until the life force they've been chowing on starts to run out, in which case they get a little gooey around the edges as things break down.

Killian and I were on our fourth memorial service of the day, chosen at random from the obituary notices and I was starting to feel a little discouraged. We hung towards the back of the funeral procession. I knew the ghoul would have enough instinct to stick around until the living types disappeared. Ghouls aren't particularly smart, but every scavenger figures out you've gotta wait for the lions to finish if you want to survive to your next meal.

Killian was looking rather dashing in his black turtleneck and jacket. Set off those baby blues of his. Just a quick trip through Austin's closet and we had ourselves a funeral appropriate genuine Armani knock off. At least I hoped it was a knock off, because I didn't know if dry cleaners would charge extra for ghoul stains. I had picked a tasteful basic black suit from Mindy's things. A dress would have been more appropriate, but it's hard taking down the undead when you're concerned about flashing your girl bits.

I touched Killian's sleeve and jerked my head away from the burial site. We walked to the far corner of the graveyard, leaving the widow to say her goodbyes and let the coffin be lowered into what, if I could help it, would be the guy's final resting place.

The drizzle was starting to come down and black umbrellas popped up everywhere. Of course it would have to be raining. Killian and I stood behind a tree. He seemed strangely quiet.

"It is a shame humans do not live for long."

"Long enough," I replied. Except for perhaps one. Dad could have stuck around for a bit longer and I wouldn't have minded at all.

We watched as the mourners paid their last respects and left arm in arm. The backhoe started covering up the stiff, but then the operator got a phone call. He turned off his machine and hopped off, walking away only halfway through the job.

"This is it."

Dusk had started to fall. Crap. Why couldn't these little beasties choose warm days on Tahitian beaches instead of muddy drizzle in an ever increasingly dark cemetery? Battling things out with the forces of darkness was always trickier when it was dark. Home court advantage and all.

"It's him."

Killian looked at me like I was nuts.

"It is the pastor."

The guy had a limp and was oozing grey tar out of his black pant leg. Unless he had come down with a rare case of flesh eating Ebola, he had an ectoplasm problem.

"I can't believe he's coming out while the undertaker is on a call."

I opened up my purse and pulled out the garlic necklaces. I looped one of them over Killian's like he was touching down in Hawaii.

"I thought you said they went after easy targets."

I shrugged, "Sometimes, they can't wait. If they haven't eaten in awhile, they'll take whatever is on the buffet table."

Killian's shoulders shook with the heebie-jeebies, "Ick."

I couldn't help but grinning. The elf was loosening up a bit.

I pulled out my magical stunning rod. I was

going to try and bring back this ghoul in one piece. Bodies with holes in them tended to leak in my trunk and I couldn't afford to get my car detailed again this month.

"Follow my lead," I said as I bent over in a crouch and ran to the first headstone. I wanted to make sure the ghoul didn't have a chance to run. Killian was right behind me on his whisper silent feet. If I ever got a boon on him, I was ordering me some of those magical elfin shoes. Maybe I'd just see if he'd give me a pair for my birthday. I looked over at him. I hoped I lasted until my next birthday.

I ran to the next gravestone and ducked behind a creepy concrete angel. I heard the pastor drop into the open grave with a squishy sound. He was decaying fast. I nodded my head to Killian to come around the other side and I rushed the hole in the ground.

There he was, the ghoul, ripping at the coffin lid like a kid trying to break into a cereal box for the prize at the bottom.

"Now what, pray tell, are you doing?"

He looked up at me and hissed. I had to fish around the grave a bit with my rod, but I got him. I huffed on my nails and buffed 'em on my shirt, "Just like that."

And then the coffin burst open and the dead

man jumped out.

Oh, he was dead all right.

But he was hungry. He grabbed that ghoul and sunk his fangs into that guy's neck so fast.

Instinctively, I reached up to my neck and felt the reassuring protection of my neckguard.

"Come on, Maggie. Do not allow him to finish feeding..."

I hated that my hands were shaking as I grabbed my silver stake from my boot top. I hurtled it right at the guy's back and it pierced it like a knitting needle in bubble wrap. He was too young a vamp to even know what killed him... you know... for the second time.

"Just like..." I suddenly became aware of a hissing sound, "...that."

I turned, edging my way to stand back to back with Killian. Vamps were dropping out of the goddamned trees. I counted eight in total. And my stake was conveniently stuck in the back of the least threatening of all of them.

"Jesus."

"Your god will not help you now," one of the undead spat at me.

"I was talking figuratively, asshole," I snapped. If it wasn't enough I was probably going to be dead in about five minutes time, it super sucked that I was about to be deaded by a bunch of dunces.

"What is the plan?" asked Killian.

"Marry rich and live on a yacht…" I muttered under my breath.

"Get us out of this, Maggie."

I scanned the group. They were trying to circle around us for the attack.

"Back up slowly towards the church. Okay, back up not so slowly and more quick like to the church," I whispered out of the side of my mouth.

"We can hear you, human," hissed the vampire

I gave him a sarcastic little smile, "Do you think I don't know that?"

I actually didn't know that, but it was nice of him to tell me.

"Killian, here's the bad news. They want us dead. My big sharpie thing is down in the grave."

"I will retrieve it."

And then he jumped in the hole to tug it out of the vampire. That's when the whole crew of suckers rushed me.

"KILLIAN! I NEED SOME HELP!"

I was able to sweep them back with my rod. I cursed myself for not buying one with anything stronger than a stunning spell. This was like one of those kung fu movies, except I wasn't Bruce Lee and I was going to be hard pressed to open up a can of whoopass. If you don't have anything pointy, vampires just keep coming. Sure, I could knock one down and break a couple arms, but they'd just hop right back up, healed and whole. If you could get over the whole soulless aspect of it all, it wasn't a bad deal being a vampire.

And I could just tell they were biding their time, wearing me out so that when they finally came in for the kill, I'd be too tired to even fight.

"KILLIAN!"

"You nailed your stake through the vamp AND the ghoul and now it is stuck in the coffin," he called up to me.

"Well, get it out!"

The vamp that rushed me looked familiar.

"WAIT! You were the widow?"

She gave me a wicked little smile.

"This was a trap? WHAT?" I sent her flying just out of spite. "How the hell were you able to come out during the daylight?"

Another funeral observer laughed a spine tingling vampire laugh at me, "Wouldn't you like to know, you spawn of Ulrich's enemy."

"How the hell do you know my uncle's name?" I said, starting to panic.

"He decided that you deserved a little welcome home present. He has always felt family is so important."

I knew better to look a vamp dead in the eye, so I just looked at him dead in the bridge of the nose, "Are you telling me my uncle consorts with vampires?"

That asshole laughed again, "Consorts? Oh my dear child, you really do have no idea what is going on."

And then that bastard came in thinking he was ready for the kill. I broke my stunning staff in two and caught the guy midflight like a Turkish shish kabob.

One stake down. And I used the other to impale a kid who looked no older than fourteen.

"Sorry, undead kid. Just think of all the acne and awkward first dates I've spared you."

I tried to yank out the stake before the next one flew at me, but I was still pulling when she landed. She looked like an evil corporate ex-cheerleader. Perfect blonde hair coiffed just right. All hairs fell right back into place every time she moved her head.

"I would have made this quick and painless for you. How shameful that you would wear garlic," she whispered.

And then the silver shaft of my stake appeared right through her heart.

Killian kicked her away, grabbed me by the wrist and we sprinted to the car, five vampires in fast pursuit.

I clicked the fob as we ran and my Honda

gave a friendly little chirp as the headlights flashed on.

We both leapt into the driver's door. I threw myself into the passenger's side and pressed the "autolock" as Killian revved the engine and pealed out, leaving the vampires in a cloud of dust.

"There was so much wrong that just happened there," I said.

The fear in Killian's eyes showed me I wasn't alone in realizing we were so fucked.

Chapter 14

We sat in a 50's themed diner just off of Sunset. I held my pathetic little glass of sweaty tap water to my swelling eye.

"How many laws of vampires did we just see ignored there?"

Killian didn't lift his eyes from the menu, "I am feeling like a strawberry shake."

I just folded up my arms and rested my head on the table, "I want out."

Killian did not seem to be grasping what I was trying to say and replied, "What are you getting? It is on me."

I couldn't believe this guy, "Peanut butter pie. A la mode."

"Good choice," he said, waving the waitress over and placing our order.

As soon as she left, I hissed, "They were in a cemetery."

Killian nodded, "Grave dirt and all."

"They aren't supposed to be on hallowed

ground."

"So somehow that church had been desecrated. Could the ghoul have done it while he was the pastor?"

I thought about it a bit and then nodded, "Yah. That could have been it."

"So the vampires have found if they can get a monster to take over the body of a holy person, they can break down the defensive barrier. It is not unheard of."

"How about vampires being out in broad daylight?"

"It was not broad daylight. It was dusk."

"Killian, we followed that funeral since 6:00PM. They were out. They are not supposed to be able to be out in sun at all."

Our food arrived and Killian tried to stall by sucking on his shake.

"Well?"

"I do not know. We shall have to find out."

"And what is this about them hanging out with my uncle? Who IS Ulrich? He is obviously more than what the fat man was saying."

"Again, I do not know."

"And do you want to know the worst part?" I almost shouted.

"Worst?"

"That ghoul is decomposing into slime in the middle of that grave meaning I don't get my skip money and I'm not going back for him, meaning my rent is not getting paid this month."

Killian laughed, "You shall be taken care of."

"YOU ARE NOT GETTING ME TO OWE YOU ANY MORE FAVORS ELF."

The entire diner stopped and looked at me.

I gulped, "I'm auditioning for a movie. We're just running lines."

Normal conversation resumed and the waitress came over, "I'm an actress, too! What are you auditioning for? I think I would make a really great elf. Was it in the breakdowns?"

I raised the glass to my eye, "I'm sorry. I'm a stunt person. I got bumped up to do a line."

She seemed disappointed and just dropped the check.

I leaned forward and whispered, "Killian, this is not good. We're not safe if the vamps can come out during the day."

"Listen, they did not attack. They stretched things out and then waited until dark which means they must not have all their power. We will go back tomorrow at noon and see what we can find. Deal?"

I sighed, "Yah. Deal."

He opened up his moneybag and pulled out several gold coins.

I placed my hand on his, "Stop. I've got it."

"I told you it was my treat."

"I'll take it out of the per diem I'm about to start charging you."

He gave me a sideways glance.

"You can't go throwing gold around here."

He looked down at his little pile of elf money, "I had forgotten that the currency is not the same as the Other Side."

I patted his hand, "It's okay, you'll just have to save my life again, okay?"

He gave me a slow half smile, "You have yourself a deal."

Chapter 15

Bed had never looked so good. I crawled into the lacy chintz goodness and nestled into the 1000 thread count sheets. I was reaching over to turn off the bedside lamp when there was a knock at the door.

"Come in?" I asked, hesitantly. I'd learned long ago that anyone knocking at your door at 11:00 at night was there for a booty call or emergency call. Sometimes both. Never neither.

Mindy came in softly and padded over to my bed, sitting at the foot of it like when we were kids.

"How'd it go today?"

I knew this was not the reason why she had come into my room. You don't spend nine months in utero with a person without being able to read their tells.

"Melted my skip, which is gonna be helluva lot of paperwork, and staked a couple vampires. Blah blah blah. You?"

She shivered, "I hate what you do."

Mindy had it rough. During school, she had gone the super brains/ballerina/cheerleader route, I think, just to get some normalcy. I hadn't been really surprised when she had gone into finance.

"Me, too. I wish I could have done anything else in the world besides this, but..."

She shrugged, "But Dad's genes."

"Yah," I humorlessly laughed, "his damned genes."

"Do you ever feel like he's still with you?"

I nodded, "Yah."

She got really quiet, "No, like, he is in the room with you. You can smell him. And you hear his footsteps like he's right behind you."

"You feeling okay?"

"No. I... It's just sometimes... it's like I catch him out of the corner of my eye, but he's not here. He's dead." She stopped and repeated, "He's dead, right?"

I sat up, "Are you saying you have Mom's gift?"

She waved her hands, "I don't know. I don't know at all. I mean, I must, because normal people don't see... Well, they don't see dead people, right?"

I shrugged, "Some swear they do."

She looked so small and scared as she

said, "With your gifts... You've always been able to do stuff that I could never do, but I have always been so glad it wasn't me. I was so glad I wouldn't have to deal with the Other Side my whole life. I have a job, a husband. I can't go living in the Other Side. I can't bring Austin over there..."

I skootched over and gave her a great big hug and didn't let go, "No one says that you do. Mom lived her whole life on Earth. Dad was the only reason..." I corrected myself, "His crazy brother was the only reason we had to live on the Other Side. And last I checked, Austin didn't have a crazy brother hunting him down."

Mindy looked at me square in the eye, "But we have a crazy uncle."

I suddenly felt very, very cold.

"You think you're responsible for all this," I stated, suddenly seeing the great big elephant she had hauled into the room.

"It makes sense, doesn't it? I start seeing dead people and you show up saying our long lost uncle has come out of the woodwork."

"No, Mindy, it doesn't. It isn't you."

"Why not?"

"Because our uncle is a deranged psychopath who is running some sort of grift on the magical community and is now involved in something that is breaking down the barriers of our two worlds.

It isn't you."

"How can you be so sure that my gift waking up isn't what started all this?"

I held her hand tightly, "I promise that you are not the start of all this. And I also promise that I will keep you and Austin safe. I didn't spend my whole life kicking asses to let yours get into trouble. As soon as this settles down, I'll take you over to Mom, or I'll bring her over, and once she finishes driving you crazy with all the pride she is about to bust out all over you, you can figure out what you're supposed to do."

"Maybe I'm going crazy."

"Maybe Dad has something important to tell you."

"Um... he's dead."

"I tell you what, next time you see him, you ask him what he wants. See what he has to say."

"I'm not going to start talking to empty rooms."

I gathered her up in my arms like we were eight years old again and some dumb boy had made her cry on the playground, "No one will think that you're stupid. You don't know if it's real or not until you try. So, try. For me?"

She nodded and then hugged me tightly, "Be safe, sis."

"You, too. Goodnight."

"Goodnight. Don't let the boogeyman bite."

"Mindy, there is no boogeyman," I said as I snuggled in to bed, "I hauled Carl in years ago."

Chapter 16

The brownie had found us, evidently. When I woke in the morning, all of my scattered clothes had been freshly laundered and folded tidily. I grabbed my robe and stumbled down to the kitchen. My sister was huddled in the breakfast nook with a baseball bat in her hand.

"Good morning!" I said, pouring myself a cup of coffee.

"WHAT THE FUCK???"

My sister didn't swear.

"What's got you so upset?"

"I came downstairs and breakfast was made and things were put away and the dishes were clean. WHAT. THE. FUCK."

"Sorry, I forgot to tell you. We battled it out with a fat elf yesterday and won ourselves a brownie. Not the chocolaty cake kind."

"There is a brownie. Here. In my Earthly

home?"

"Yep."

"Oh." She started to unfold, "Well, that was very kind of him… to help…"

I gave her a wink, "Thought you might enjoy."

"Why didn't you tell me, you jerk?" she said, throwing a carefully folded napkin at my head and taking a plate over to the island to snag a bear claw from the pile of pastries.

"It completely slipped my mind. He's helping me find Ulrich."

"Do you remember when we were kids? We would have done anything for a brownie."

"Don't say I never got you nothing."

"I think Christmas is covered," she said, biting into the pastry. "Oh god, this is so good. I think he made it himself."

"I wouldn't doubt it."

Killian came out, scratching his messy nest of hair and looking entirely too sexy for 8AM, "I see the brownie found us."

"They tend to be good like that."

Killian grabbed a piece of fruit from a bowl and bit into it, "I have missed nectar."

"Here the brownie goes to all this trouble to brew up some coffee and get us some sugary goodness and you're all excited about fruit? Elf, you and I may not be on speaking terms."

"You are not getting rid of me that easily," he laughed, "I have far more annoying habits to repulse you with."

"Great. I can hardly wait."

"So, what's your plan for today?" asked my sister.

"I figure we'll talk to the brownie, see if he has any good leads, investigate them, and try not to get killed."

"Sounds like a great plan. I shall be in the shower," Killian said, planting a kiss on the top of my head.

"He's cute," said my sister, watching him walk down the hall.

"Not that cute."

"I wouldn't kick him out of bed for eating grapes."

I rolled my eyes.

Chapter 17

Before Killian and I could finish buckling our seatbelts, Pipistrelle opened the door and popped into the backseat. I focused the rearview mirror so that I could see him better, "Thanks for breakfast, Pipistrelle. Any good news?"

"Indeed! Your uncle is here in the city of Angels," he replied.

"We knew that."

"I have no further information," he stated in his chirpy little voice.

I turned to Killian, "Really? This is what the Fat Man thought would help us?"

Killian shrugged, "It really was a terribly good breakfast."

I looked back at Pipistrelle, "Thanks for the food. Keep looking for my uncle."

Pipistrelle's face broke into a grin, "Indeed! Nothing would please me more!"

His little head disappeared from view and I saw the door open and shut.

"You don't think he's dragging his feet so that he can hang out with us longer?" I asked.

Killian shook his head, bemused.

I turned on the car and started backing out of the driveway, "Well, time to head to the graveyard and pick up whatever pieces of that ghoul are left so that I can collect my bounty and pay my rent. Hope it's safe to return."

"It is broad daylight," Killian reassured.

"I hope that's still enough to protect us."

We pulled up next to the church. The backhoe was just where the undertaker had left it. The bodies of the vampires had "magically" disappeared, though.

I parked my car and we walked through the crunching leaves to the graveside. The ghoul's empty clothes lay spread eagle on the coffin and green slime dripped from where his body should have been.

I dunno. I've stared at a million corpses and you get kind of used to it. Other Siders are creatures of ether and usually, when they die on Earth, their bodies poof out and they return to the dimension from whence they came.

But ghouls are gross. Being as they attain their shape through eating dead flesh, when they die you get a lingering smell that can only be described as foul. Rotting flesh squared. I pulled out a facemask and rubber gloves that I had learned to start carrying in my bag and put them on.

"Keep a lookout for me," I said to Killian and leapt into the grave.

I pulled out a plastic Ziploc bag and started folding up the clothes when something in the ghoul's jean's pocket fell out.

"Well, what do we have here?"

It was a tarnished silver bracelet with a number of lovely little charms featuring unholy artifacts hanging from its chain. I dropped it into a secondary bag.

"What did you find?" asked Killian.

"I have no idea what you're talking about."

"That bracelet you just dropped into the baggie."

"Well, Killian, there is no bracelet and there is no second baggie. But if such a thing existed, I would have to say it was a talisman of some sort."

I threw the baggie up at Killian, which he caught midair and held up to the sun to get a better look.

"This one charm looks like a coat of arms..." He suddenly got very still.

"What?"

"I believe it is your family's coat of arms."

I didn't even know we had a family coat of arms, much less what it looked like. I'm pretty sure that maybe once we had gone into one of those genealogy t-shirt shops you find at the mall, but I seem to remember coming up empty handed. Sucked that the first time I was going to see my family crest was when it was removed from the body of the undead, "Great. Think I could get it printed on a mug?"

Killian gave me a look.

"It would make the holidays easy," I explained.

Killian shook his head.

I sighed and dropped the last of the ghoul's slimy clothes in the bag. Killian lent me a hand and I climbed up the side of the grave and out.

I wandered over to my car, pulled out a briefcase, and went back to the gravesite. I opened up the briefcase and grabbed a sports bottle from inside. I popped the sippy top and sprinkled the water on the grave in the sign of a cross.

"What...?" Killian asked.

"Have to re-consecrate the ground. I've got a priest I know who can come give us a hand, but it's better to get this party started before word gets out to the nasties that there is an open church for rent. Could you fire up that backhoe for me?"

Killian flipped the keys to "on" as I sprinkled more water on the fill dirt. I climbed up into the machine and began finishing the job of laying the poor schmoe's empty coffin to rest.

"I like a woman who knows how to handle heavy machinery."

"Don't make me bury you alive."

"Just in case you were keeping tally."

I wiped my dirty hands on my pants, "What do you say we take a stroll over to the church there so that I can wash up?"

Killian nodded and followed me over, opening up the door.

The church inside was eerily quiet. Not peaceful quiet. Church quiet should make you want to rest and just be. This was the kind of quiet that makes you check your locks.

There was a summoning circle set up by the altar and the whole place smelled like rotten eggs. I kept my hand upon my stake and walked in, "Yah, the priest was definitely the first to go."

I popped open my cell phone and scrolled through my contacts until I came to the one I was looking for. The phone rang a couple times before a familiar voice growled at me from the other side.

"Father Killarney! It's Maggie... You got a second? Seems like St. Bartholomew's is in need of a little holy help... Yes, I will buy you dinner."

I snapped my phone shut, "He's on his way over. We should probably check to make sure there isn't anything hiding in the baptismal font."

The font was filled with leaves and dirt and sludge.

"Great," I said as I grabbed one of those long, brass thingies they use to light candles and poked the handle around the bottom of the font, "Someone has been using it as a bathtub."

Nothing leapt out to eat my face, so I called it good and moved on to the next spot ghoulies like to linger.

The sacristy had been cracked open and the wafers left out, eaten like crackers next to a goblet filled with something I didn't even want to consider.

"Looks like the vampires made themselves at home."

Killian looked repulsed, which was appropriate if you hadn't seen anything like this before. I don't know what it said about me that I was unfazed.

"This priest you know, he can set this wrongness right?" he asked.

"Yah, he's got a regular Sunshine Cleaning crew. They'll get this place spic and span in a jiffy."

We hung around straightening up the mess that we could until the door opened and a short, grey-haired priest interrupted our fun. He lugged a duffel bag over his shoulder. Behind him came a middle aged nun in a blue habit, rolling a roadies case.

"Well, if it isn't my dear Maggie MacKay. Haven't been seeing you in church lately," the priest said in his sweet Irish lilt.

"You know how it goes jumping between worlds, Father Killarney," I said, giving him a hug.

"The Lord only asks one hour of our time a week, my child."

I waved at the nun behind him, a slender lady with dirty blonde bangs and a wide grin. She gave me a wry glance.

"Sister Magdalena. How come you always get stuck with the heavier bag?"

"I'm just lucky."

I turned to Killian, "Killian, this is Father Killarney and Sister Magdalena. They're our cleanup crew."

Handshakes were given all around before we broke off to give them the tour.

Father Killarney put on rubber gloves and crouched down next to a circle in the floor. He brushed aside the black sand, "Well, nothing too complicated."

He then stopped and smelled his fingers, "Well, this is unfortunate."

I bent down beside him, and then shifted as I

felt Killian's eyes gazing adoringly at my backside.

Elves.

"What?" I asked Father Killarney.

"Brimstone."

"Excuse me?"

"Sulfur, but burned in the Other Side in order to transport things here."

"Meaning?"

"They built their own portal."

"Fuck."

Father Killarney gave me a chiding look.

"Sorry. Crap."

He gave me another look.

"I am very upset about this, okay?"

"Perhaps if you weren't so noticeably absent from Sunday services, you would find other ways to express your dismay."

"Sister Magdalena, do I really have to put up with this?"

She pulled the last pieces of an industrial strength, evil sucking vacuum out of the case and plugged it into the wall.

"Don't look at me. I have to put up with him every day," she said as she snapped a black dust mask over her mouth in punctuation.

"Would you expound on the meaning of the circle?" asked Killian, deflecting the heat for me and getting this party back on track.

Father Killarney nodded, getting out of the

way for Sister Magdalena to suck up the runes that had been poured out on the floor.

"Killian, the ability to jump between worlds is a valuable gift and most are not as fortunate as your girlfriend Maggie here."

"I'm not his girlfriend."

"It would do you some good, child."

Killian nodded his head gravely in agreement, "He is a man of God, Maggie..."

"Shut up."

Father Killarney cleared his throat, "As I was saying, you can jump to this world with various runes and spells. This particular spell was put together with black magic on the Other Side using brimstone to hold the portal open. Once lit, it burns in both dimensions. The trouble, as you know, is that once you are here, it is very difficult to go back."

I completed his thought, "So if there are vampires jumping over here under the radar, they are permanent guests."

Father Killarney put a finger to his nose and pointed at me. While I normally would have hoped that this was the universal sign for "we'd make great charade partners", I knew he meant I was dead on.

"So how long ago do you think they were here working the original spell?"

Father Killarney scratched his beard, "Well, the runes were still fairly fresh. Wind and dust hadn't blown them too hard, which is fortunate enough. Tracking down sulfur in the cracks and crevasses of a stone floor is one of my least favorite things to do."

Sister Magdalena lifted her mask, "As if he's ever the one tracking it down. Father, you can work while you talk."

He made the sign of the cross, "Forgive her, Father, for she knows not what she does."

She shook her head and continued to vacuum.

"My professional guess is that they have been squatting in this unholy place no more than a few days," he said.

I gave a low whistle, "Just a few days, huh?"

"Time is the enemy when you do not wish for people to find out what you are doing."

"There were a lot of vampires for a couple 24 hour shifts."

"Perhaps they were here before," offered Sister Magdalena.

And that's when I got the heebie-jeebies. I thought to the silver bracelet sitting in the baggie, "And my uncle is tied up in this mess somehow. Why can't my family just be quiet, law abiding citizens?"

Father Killarney sighed, "To every light there

must be a dark. To every yin, a yang. Your uncle's wicked ways are only a balance to the good of your father."

"Sibling rivalry must've been a bitch."

He laughed, "Indeed, it was."

I looked at Father Killarney, "Wait. You knew my uncle?"

"Indeed, I did. I knew him until the day that he turned away from us."

"What do you think he is up to?" I asked, gazing around at the death and mayhem of a place that should have been filled with light and life.

"I assume he is looking for you."

"What?" I asked him sharply. "Why would he be looking for me?"

"I assume because you are the only one who can put a stop to this."

"That's a random statement to lay on a girl."

Father Killarney and Killian shared an unspoken, pointed moment and I kind of didn't want to find out what they were so rudely not telling me.

Killian finally turned to me, "Maggie, I was sent to you to find out why the barrier was weakening. I was told it was because you were the only one who could fix it." He waved at the mess in the church, "But now, if your uncle is at the root of this matter... Perhaps it is because your blood runs thicker than water."

"Great," I said, pressing my palms into my increasingly throbbing temples. "I'm supposed to magically know something about a man that I'd never heard of before a couple days ago and save the world with said information."

"That's about the color of things," said Father Killarney, completely unhelpfully.

"You can fill me in on the guy anytime now," I pointedly requested.

He gently guided me and Killian to the door, "I will. I promise, child. But this abomination upon holy ground must be sorted out before sundown. Go. Get lunch. Watch some afternoon talk shows. I shall tell you everything this evening."

Father Killarney was an expert in cleaning up bad magic. He'd seen far worse than what mine eyes had gazed upon, and that was saying something. If he was subtly suggesting that he had to get down to brass tacks, then he needed to get started. I grudgingly decided that I could let him worry about the end of the world for a couple hours.

I hugged him warmly. Father Killarney used to eat at our Sunday night dinners back before all hell had broken loose and we had to move across the boundary. He was one of the good guys. I waved at Sister Magdalena who saluted me farewell with her hose.

Killian and I walked back to the car, picking our way through the dead grass and headstones. Fall didn't really come to Los Angeles, but every now and again, you'd find a misplaced maple amidst the eucalyptus and palm trees. For some reason, this church featured some stunted oaks to help tell the change between the seasons.

I stood at my car, staring back at the church. Doing nothing for the afternoon just didn't sit right. I couldn't let it go.

"Killian? We found out about the funeral from an obituary in the paper. Maybe it's time to pay a visit to the funeral director..."

Killian gave me a smile.

"Besides," I said, unlocking the door, "there's nothing on since they staked Jerry Springer."

Chapter 18

The funeral home was a white clapboard sided thing with black shutters and a curved driveway. Sort of a grim Georgian rancher left over from the prefab homes of the 1950s. It had a utilitarian, matter-of-factness to it that fit in well with the blue-collar neighborhood.

We walked in the front door. Inside, the industrial carpet was a delightful shade of turquoise green and the place smelled of floral deodorizer.

There was a red door with a slide-y sign in black plastic that read "Director". I knocked gently and the door swung open.

The director's desk sat empty.

"No one seems to be home," I remarked.

We stood in silence for a moment.

"I suppose the polite thing to do would be to wait inside his office for him to return."

"That seems like the only polite thing," replied Killian.

"Perhaps you'd like to wait outside the door in case he returns."

"I think perhaps I would."

I slipped inside and began searching through the tidily stacked papers on his desk. In his outbox, I found an invoice for yesterday's service. I didn't want to screw over the guy. I know what a pain it is when you're sure you left an important paper somewhere, so I just copied down the billing information and then slipped back out into the hall.

"Did you see him?"

"Not a soul," said Killian.

We stood there for a few more moments.

"This is strange, isn't it? Just that the door would be open, his office would be open, and no one would be here..." I got that old heebie-jeebie feeling again, "We have to go down and check the mortuary, don't we?"

I could see Killian didn't like it any more than me, "Yes, I believe we do."

Crap."

I unholstered my gun and palmed a stake. We walked to the end of the hall and pressed the elevator button going down.

The doors opened with a ding.

We exited into a white morgue, cold storage lockers fitted into the walls.

"You as creeped out as I am?" I asked.

"Yes," he replied.

All the lights were on, but no one appeared to be home.

I walked over to the first locker and pulled on the handle. It was locked, but I didn't see a keyhole.

"I can't open it."

Killian came over and had no more luck than I did on any of the units.

"Well," I said. "It appears to be a dead end." I looked over at Killian, "I am COMPLETELY okay with that."

"As am I," he said, his shoulders relaxing below his earlobes for the first time since we came into the basement.

"I guess we do have an afternoon free to fill up with bad talk shows after all."

"It sounds more appealing with each passing moment."

We started walking towards the elevator and, out of my little green energy habit, I flipped the lights off.

And that was when I heard every single one of those sixteen cold storage lockers open at once and the sound of sixteen tray tables slide out.

"Fuck!"

I flipped on the light.

Sitting up in each of the tray tables was

a dead person. Except, not dead anymore. Vampires. Young, hungry vampires. Older vampires have a little more wisdom and maturity to their undead years. The young ones were missing basic table manners, like, "Don't eat your guests."

In unison, they hissed and then were coming at us.

I banged at the "up" button but the elevator door was not opening. I swung around and caught a vamp with my stake as I grabbed a scalpel from a table and plunged it into the heart of another.

"Killian, there are too many of them!"

I grabbed Killian and we ran up the steps of the emergency exit. I sure wished the fire marshal had a nice little "in case of vampire attack, break glass" box, but we were on our own. I fired off a round and it connected with something that was coming at us fast.

We ran out onto the first floor, tore down the hall, and made it outside into the safety of daylight.

"WHAT THE FUCK??!" I shouted, breathing heavily.

Killian looked at his arm. He had a scrape that was bleeding pretty good. I brought him over to the car and pulled out a first aid kit, "They get you?"

He shook his head, "I am merely grazed."

I got him wrapped up and gave him a sympathetic pat.

Then, I pulled out a tourniquet tube from the kit and popped open my gas tank. After a quick search around the back of the building, I found a watering can that the gardener forgot to put away. Probably because something tried to eat him.

The surgeon general warns not to do this, but with a couple sucks, I had the gas flowing through the tube into the watering can at a steady rate. Thank god I filled up before we left. I carried the can over to the funeral home and sprinkled it everywhere I could find. I then took out a match and flicked it at the building.

It went up like a roman candle.

Killian stood next to me as we watched the place burn down like the Atlanta scene in *Gone with the Wind*, "We should probably leave before we're spotted."

"Let's hope the South doesn't rise again," I replied.

Chapter 19

We drove the car off the top of Mulholland drive and back into the Other Side with a thump. I wound my way through the cobblestone streets to the police station.

I walked into the holding office and plunked the baggy full of drippy clothes on Lacy's desk.

"Sorry, I'm afraid I caught him more dead than alive."

She gave me a heavy sigh, "Do you know the extra paperwork this is going to cause me?"

"That's why they pay you the big bucks, Lacy."

She got up and sashayed her way over to the register to fill out my proof of vanished-but-still-taken-care-of corpse delivery.

"Hey, Lacy?" I asked.

"Hmm?" she replied.

"Any word on weird stuff going on with the vampires?"

She ripped out the receipt and brought it

over to me, "You been living under a rock?"

"Evidently. What's going on?"

"New leader just took over. Something about promises to unite them and restore them to a position of pride and dignity. Blah blah blah."

"Huh. So who is this leader?"

"Vampires aren't too forthcoming about giving names and, personally, I try not to spend too much time in their company," she said as she placed a meaningful blue finger on my shoulder.

"Lacy, when did you get shy?" I replied. "You've always been my ear to the ground. My person-in-the-know. My go-to-hell gal. I need you to live on the edge."

She grabbed a stack of papers and plunked them in front of me, "And I need you to fill all this out in triplicate and return it to me by close-of-business Friday."

Lacy sure knew how to ruin a gal's day. I should have let those vampires turn me. I wouldn't have to fill out the twenty-page Form 168A staring up at me.

Lacy leaned her elbows on her desk, "Listen, you didn't hear it from me, but you should head down to the Wagon and Cock. They always seem to know what's going on."

"Thanks, Lacy. What would I do without you?"

"Die."

"That's about right."

I stepped into the car and turned on the engine.

"Any good word?" asked Killian.

"Got a nice little lead," I replied. "How about you let me buy you a drink?"

Chapter 20

The Wagon and Cock was a tavern down by the waterfront. It had a rougher element, but you don't find out what's going on in the seedy underbelly of a city by hanging out at debutante balls.

That said, I made sure I was fully armed before going inside. I popped open my glove compartment and handed Killian a Glock.

"I do not use guns."

"Who said it was for you?"

He raised an eyebrow.

"Listen, some ladies make men carry their purses. All I'm asking is for you to carry my extra gun."

He watched as a six armed sailor lit up three cigars and leaned against the light pole outside the pub, puffing each cigar in turn.

"Rough crowd?"

"You could strike a match off their aura."

I slammed the last cartridge into place and tucked my own firearm into the top of my boot.

"Alrighty, then. Let's do this."

Heads turned as I walked into the pub and then went back to drowning their sorrows in the depths of their grog. I walked up to the bar and gave the bartender a nice down payment on his vacation home.

"This round's on me!" I announced.

Instantly, the entire place was filled with my best friends. Showy? Yes. But muddled heads loosened tongues, and that's what I needed.

I turned to the bar keeper as he tried to hand me some change, "Keep it. Actually, keep it and here's some more for that entire bottle you've got there on the top shelf."

He gave me a grunt and handed over something that would put hair on the chest of a two year old, and turned back to his duties.

Obstacle one hurdled.

I slid over to a solitary fellow who looked a bit anemic.

"Had a bit of good luck and I hate drinking alone. Mind if I joined you?" I asked.

He eyed Killian, "Looks like you have more than enough to drink with."

I topped off his half filled glass and poured myself a shot, "He keeps to the nectar and that's not quite my idea of a celebration, if you know what I mean."

The fellow lifted his glass and clinked it to my own.

"What's your name?" I asked.

"Pour me another and I'll tell you."

"You're my kind of fellow."

The thing about drinking with a guy like this is that you've got to take the first couple shots for the team, but still make sure to keep a clear enough head to not get yourself killed. Killian was my backup plan. The Wagon and Cock wasn't a place for getting sloppy. I had a few too many enemies this side of the boundary to let my guard down too much.

"My name is Lars."

"Nice enough name, Lars. I'm Maggie."

We shook hands and I poured us both another. I let him throw his back while I spilled mine down my front.

"What's your line of business?" I asked.

"Little of this. Little of that. You?"

"I am a merchant," I lied, "specializing in multi-world transportation of sensitive objects."

"From the way you're spreading money around, I'd fancy you're doing well for yourself."

"I keep a roof over my head."

An accordion player struck up a tune in the corner. The fact accordion players existed in one world, much less two, was a cruel and unusual punishment, I felt, but Lars seemed to enjoy the music and it covered over the awkward moments in our conversation a bit.

"It's the strangest thing," I said. "Business has been dropping off. I heard there are some new portals opening up between the worlds."

"Can't say I've heard of anything."

"Huh. Something about a new head of the vampires?"

"That information, missy," Lars said as he rose from the table, "is worth more than the expensive bottle you've got held in your hands there."

I rose and met his blurry eyes. Sometimes you have to ask nice. And sometimes you have to let people know that your breasts aren't going to get in the way of you kicking their ass.

"Seems funny a big strong man like yourself is running scared. I just asked a simple question."

"Your simple question gets a person like me killed."

"No need to get angry, sir. I was just looking for a name. Like I said, I'm a runner and I'm looking for some employment opportunities."

"Employment opportunities?" He leaned in to me, "Fine. The vamp's name is Vaclav. He keeps his human minions here at the harbor, over at

Pier 67. And if you asked me, I'd tell you to stay as far away as you possibly can. Business can't ever be bad enough to work for that one. But you seem the type hell-bent on finding out how fast you can die, so enjoy your final days."

And then Lars took off with a limp, fixing his cap upon his head and heading out the door.

"That went well," said Killian as we watched him go.

"More info than we had when we came in," I replied as I slammed the cork back into the expensive bottle and dropped it in front of a pirate passed out at the table next to us. Not quite hidden treasure, but he was going to wake up feeling like a lucky man.

"So, do we head off to Pier 67?" asked Killian.

"Killian, I'm foolhardy, but I'm not an idiot." I rose and walked to the door, "We wait until morning."

Perhaps if I hadn't been such an idiot, I would have noticed that the bar keeper had been watching the entire exchange.

Chapter 21

Night had fallen and my head was pounding.

"Can I get you anything?" I shouted to Killian in the other room as I put my cup underneath the faucet. Sobering while I was still awake was my least favorite feeling.

Coming out of the haze, though, made me look twice at the shadow that danced across my lawn. Ah, it was so good to be home. I pulled my gun out of the kitchen island.

"Killian! We've got company!"

I shut off the lights. If they were nasties, lights wouldn't be the thing keeping them in or out. If they weren't nasties, I was going to take any advantage I could grab hold of.

"What do you see?" he whispered at my elbow. He had ditched his staff in favor of a crossbow. Excellent choice.

"Something is moving out there in the dark."

Another shadow flitted across the lawn, coming closer to the house stealthily. I could now rule out the neighbor's cat.

I stretched my fingers, trying not to let the heady rush of adrenaline make me shoot till I saw the reds of their eyes.

"Why do you look like you are enjoying this?" asked Killian.

"Better than a cup of coffee to wake a girl up."

"Remind me never to wake you up."

"Done."

Now something dropped silently out of a tree and into the yard.

"Okay, so that makes three. Goll, why do they always have to attack on the new moon?"

"Avoiding the reflection of the sun...?"

"It was rhetorical."

"Sorry."

"Okay, you can cover the front, garage, and back door if you stand where I am here in the kitchen," I said. "I'm going upstairs to check the windows."

He gave me a nod and I made my way in a low crouch to the stairs.

From the second floor, I counted five vamps surrounding the house. Vampires are nasty, but the good thing about the Other Side is that homes are protected against this sort of thing. I holstered my gun and walked downstairs.

"Just vamps."

Killian relaxed, "Good."

I started laughing, "Don't you love it when it's

'just vampires'?"

Killian gave a rueful chuckle, "Yes."

Suddenly I heard a voice calling loudly, "Maggie! Maggie MacKay! We bring a message for you."

I took a second to think it through, but decided it was probably worth it for me to find out what they were doing here. I jerked my head towards the backdoor.

Killian raised his crossbow, "After you, milady."

I opened my door, but left my screen door closed. Technically, the threshold of my home should have held at the porch steps, but flying projectiles don't have the restrictions of thresholds and I wasn't going to expose myself any more than I had to.

"What do you want, vampire?"

"Come out and talk?"

"Don't insult me."

"Or you could let us come in to you."

"Or I could shut the door and spend the rest of the night reading a good book. I'm standing here listening, which is more than your undead ass deserves."

"We bring a message of peace."

"Right."

"We could go get some associates of ours that

are not bound by the sanctity of your home."

"Would you quit the pissing competition and tell me what it is you need to tell me? I've got a bathtub that needs scrubbing."

"You were looking for answers at the Wagon and Cock this evening..."

My ears pricked up, "I have no idea what you're talking about."

"The man you spoke with is already dead for the information he shared."

Crap. I never meant to get anyone killed. I didn't want to get anyone killed by a vampire. I rubbed my neckguard. I knew what that fate felt like.

"If I was talking to someone, and I'm not saying I was, what concern of it is yours?"

I heard the vampires hissing at each other there in the darkness before coming to silent agreement, "The night has ears..."

I was going to have to go out. I owed the dead Lars that much. I turned to Killian and he could evidently see the decision on my face. One didn't get very far in the tracking business if one wasn't willing to take chances. You also didn't get very far if you were a blithering fool. I went over to my coat closet and pulled out some Kevlar.

Killian straightened my vest in a very proprietary way and laid his hands on my neckguard, "If the vampires attempt an attack, I shall, as you would say, 'drop them' before they can get past this, my partner."

I gave him a grim nod and then stepped out of the house. Killian's crossbow was trained on the leader. I walked to the corner of the porch.

"What?" I asked.

The leader walked forward, "We are... grateful... for your willingness to meet with us."

"I wouldn't call this willingness."

"We need you to create a portal for us."

I laughed, "Oh, you vampires are rich..."

"Yes, we are."

And that was when he dropped a sack of money that was filled with probably ten years worth of my salaries in one burlap wrapped sum.

I looked at him in disbelief, "You've got some talking to do."

"We need you to build a portal."

"Yah, that's why god invented the legal channels. It'll save you a whole bunch of dough."

"The 'legal' channels are being monitored by our master. It is how we have known when you left the Other Side and when you returned. We know things about your uncle."

"What do you know about my uncle?" I asked sharply.

"He has promised a harvest of humans from Earth."

My uncle was sounding like a better and better guy every time I learned something new about him. I could see why my dad decided to strand him on Earth.

"Listen, if you're bent out of shape because my uncle broke some promise about an all-you-can-eat human buffet and think I'm going to build you some interdimensional drive-thru window, you're barking up the wrong crazy tree, Mr. Crazy."

The vampire hissed in frustration, "You do not understand. He is working with the new master. We..." the vampire motioned to his associates, "do not subscribe to Vaclav's views and wish to disrupt the flow."

"And which views exactly is it that you don't subscribe to?"

"The humans are not being captured to feed our clan. They are being turned to grow our numbers. Vaclav seeks to collapse the boundary between worlds. To do so puts us all at risk. It is not sustainable. We have information that if delivered tonight could put an end to this plan."

"So you magically show up on my doorstep, just a bunch of secret spy vampires, and want me to open up a portal so that you can head over to Earth and put an end to your master's greedy ways? I haven't heard a story that lame since I quit babysitting teenagers."

"You are our only hope."

"Go home. I don't work with vampires."

And with that, I turned and walked to the house.

"We will be dead by tomorrow," said the leader vampire.

"And why should I care?"

"Our master believes your uncle is his partner and weakens the barrier for a common cause. But your uncle is plotting his own war. Both sides will destroy each other if the barrier comes down. Pier 67 holds the answers. You must go there tomorrow."

"Why?" I asked, barely looking over my shoulder.

"A jade artifact will be brought in to help transport our kind between the two worlds. It is in the shape of a Chinese lion. You must protect it from your uncle and our master."

I gave a shrug, "I'll check it out."

"Maggie MacKay, do not be a fool. We come here knowing the risk, knowing to do so would seal our doom. Listen to what we are saying to you."

I spun, "No, you listen to me, vamp. I've fallen for your people's goodwill more than once. This isn't the first time I have been approached on a matter of direst consequence. I listened to your lies once and it almost got me killed. I will look into your ridiculous jade lion and if I find there is some merit to what you say, I will handle it. But don't you dare come marching into my backyard, telling me you need a portal and then try to play the guilt card on me. I'm not playing. I know your kind."

I walked back into the house and slammed the door behind me, stopping to lean against the kitchen island and catch my breath.

Killian's gentle hand was at my waist. I probably should have shaken him off, but sometimes even someone like me just needs to know someone cares.

He pulled me close to him and I leaned against is broad chest. He rested his cheek upon the top of my head.

"Why does it always have to be vampires?" I muttered into his shirt.

"There, there. We bagged a ghoul. It is not always vampires."

Thank god for elves.

Chapter 22

I woke to the sun shining. I could smell cinnamon and coffee coming from the kitchen and stumbled my way down the stairs.

Killian came over and planted a kiss on my forehead before handing me a mug of deep black coffee, "So, today we check out Pier 67?

"Yah. That and I need to do some research on a jade lion."

I opened up the cupboard to pull out some plates and then noticed that Killian had already set the table. Someone's mama raised him right. It had been a long time since anyone had cooked me breakfast with no bikini strings attached.

I took a seat and helped myself to some sort of gooey coffee cake roll thing with icing and butter. Man, he was a good cook.

"Do you believe that the vampires were telling the truth?" he asked.

I tried to focus on the question and not the fact his cooking was better than the majority of the intimate relationships I had been in.

I swallowed and washed down that little bit of heaven with some coffee, "Listen, vampires look out for themselves. I haven't met one who breaks with that tradition. If those guys were being honest that bringing down that barrier is going to cause personal problems, sure, they could've been telling the truth. But I would place my money on 'hungry'." I pointed at the food, "If I was starving and I knew all I had to do was drop some cash on the doorstep of some dumb broad who could work portals..."

I stopped eating, the food suddenly tasting like putty, "How did they know I could work portals?" I threw down my fork, "My uncle has a fat mouth."

Killian sat down and placed his napkin on his lap like a grown-up. "Your uncle is looking for you, and it makes sense he would warn them you have that ability."

I turned to Killian and gave him a grim smile, "Here's the plan. We go to the docks while it's daylight and check things out. And then we jump worlds. In case it's true that the official portals are being watched, I'll take us through a portal the officials don't know about. And then we find my uncle. And then we end him."

Killian took the coffee out of my hand, "I shall collect my things."

Chapter 23

The docks were as I always remembered them. The wood was silvery gray and the piers were covered in Other Side barnacles, which had a nasty habit of not being the nice, passive little creatures you find over on Earth.

Killian stuck close by my side, close enough that occasionally we would bump into one another. I didn't complain.

We got to Pier 67. The warehouse's windows were all blacked out and a heavy chain locked the door closed. I didn't see anyone, so I pulled a crowbar out of the back of my trunk and made my way to one of the windows.

"Do you think it is wise?"

"Nope," I replied as I jimmied up the window. If there was an alarm, we had minutes before security arrived. If there had been magical protection, we'd already be dead.

But when I popped open the window, I didn't see or hear anything.

"Give me a lift up, will you?"

Killian stuck his head between my legs and picked me up like we were at a concert on the 4th of July instead of breaking into a warehouse.

"You could have just given me a lift with your hands," I muttered.

"Your shoes have stepped in every manner of Other Side muck," he replied. "Plus, this is more fun."

I kicked him lightly in the ribs. Fun. Totally my thoughts on the day.

"Do you see anything?" he asked.

The inside of the warehouse was filled with crates, floor to ceiling. There was some sort of writing on each of them. Looked Chinese, but my eastern character identification skills were not particularly honed.

I pulled myself up, Sweating to the Oldies eat your heart out, and dropped inside.

"Want to find something to pull me over?" Killian called.

I couldn't believe this elf. Not knowing what was in here and shouting like that. Yes, we were probably okay if jimmying open the window and crawling inside hadn't set off any alarms, but just because something appeared to be too easy didn't mean it actually was. Sometimes people made it easy by booby-trapping a place. And, yes, sometimes they were just idiots.

"Stand watch!" I hissed.

I heard a loud rumble ricochet through the warehouse. I pressed myself flat against the wall. The coast clear, I somersaulted across the concrete and hid behind a stack of crates.

The sound came again.

And then I realized what it was.

Snoring.

Someone was frickin' sleeping on the job. I crept towards the center of the warehouse and the glow of an industrial scoop light. Slumped in some old, battered chairs by a wooden desk were three beef-headed trolls, the club-first-ask-questions-later type. They were out so cold they were drooling on their shirts.

By their snoozing bodies were six empty pizza boxes. I lifted one of the lids. Someone had spiked it with toadstools, a fact three hungry trolls would have overlooked. That's the problem with interspecies security. Yah, they could crush a car with their fist but they are dumb as a box of rocks.

But speaking of dumb, I would be an idiot if I ignored the fact someone had drugged a gaggle of trolls. Said people probably had an interest in what was going on at Pier 67, and, most likely, would be along shortly to take advantage of said window of opportunity. You know. If they weren't already here.

I started riffling through the papers on the desk. Packing receipts, invoices, bladdity blah. And then I came across one that gave me a little shiver down my spine. "Stacked cold storage units" and the name of the funeral home I had set on fire. Good times.

I looked over at the massive canyon of crates surrounding me. None of them appeared to be big enough to hold units like we saw in the morgue. I muttered a silent prayer that the powers of dark hadn't invented a shrink ray and squished a bunch of mini-vampires into the boxes.

I just about came out of my skin as a hand rested on my shoulder.

"Maggie?"

"WHAT THE FUCK KILLIAN! YOU DO NOT SNEAK UP ON ME EVER AGAIN!" I whisper-shouted at him. I swear to god, I may have had a heart attack. "How the hell did you get in here?"

"The back door was open."

Great, I went breaking and entering when I could have just wandered in the back door. It answered my question about whether the visitors were already here or on their way. Looks like we just missed them.

"Listen," I said, "you go search around the warehouse and see if you spot trouble. I'm going to keep looking through files. Hoot like an owl if we're about to die."

The trolls appeared to still be sawing logs like W.C. Fields after too many cups of eggnog. Still, I carefully tiptoed as I continued my paper search.

"What do we have here?" I mused as I looked at an invoice. "Lion. Jade. Arrival time 10:45AM."

That was about a half hour before we showed up. It had been signed for, too.

I looked over at the trolls.

"Who knocked you out..." I wondered out loud.

I heard the owl hoot and took off at a sprint.

Turned out to be a false alarm.

"I told you to hoot like an owl if you were in trouble."

Killian grimaced, "This, my dear Maggie, is most definitely trouble."

He pointed to a circle of intricate designs laid out in the ground like the one in the church.

"An illegal portal," I said as I crouched down. I scuffed my foot across the brimstone dust, breaking the circle and rendering it useless.

"Probably trying to move some goods over to Earth. Specifically, this," I said as I held out the invoice.

Killian took it out of my hand, "Jade lion. It appears the vampires were telling the truth."

"But from the looks of things, someone

double crossed someone."

"How do you know that?"

I pointed at a note that had been stabbed into the side of a wooden crate with a nasty looking knife.

"I'm guessing that's not a love letter."

Killian reached up to take it.

"STOP!"

He raised his hands in apology.

"We want the bad guys to be mad at the right people. We just need to glean what info we can before they show up."

Killian stood on his tiptoes, "It reads, 'Your reign of terror is at an end' and then it has a symbol."

I ran back to the desk and stole a quill and the ink well. I ran back to the crate and sketched the symbol on the back of my hand. Satisfied I pretty much captured the gist of the mark, I turned to Killian, "I know a guy who is an expert in symbols."

"Back to Earth?"

"Back, my friend, to Earth."

Chapter 24

As soon as we arrived, I found a payphone and dialed Father Killarney's home number. I was starting to feel kinda nervous about using my cell. Since the vamps appeared to not have been lying about the lion, I was getting a little spooked that maybe they were telling the truth about the official portal monitoring. That, in turn, gave me the old heebie-jeebies about what else they might possibly be tapping.

"Father Killarney? ...yes, I will try to go to church on Sunday... Yes... I know..." I sat there silently listening as he read me the riot act about my eternal soul. Finally, I just interrupted, "Listen, I owe you a meal. Can I take you right now? You and Sister Magdalena?"

He got right friendly after that. We made arrangements and about an hour later were sitting in a pub with some pints, listening to a three-piece band, and waiting on our fish and chips orders.

Sister Magdalena was turning my hand in

hers to get a better look at the drawing. Father Killarney's itched his chin thoughtfully, "Well, it is not exactly like what I've seen before."

"I was in a rush. I might have missed a couple strokes."

Sister Magdalena assured me, "You got the heart of it. The closest match I have seen is an old elfin signature."

Father Killarney nodded his head in agreement, "Perhaps the Shadow Elves?"

I gave Killian a steely glance, "You holding out on me, partner?"

He held up his palms in innocence.

Shadow Elves were a loose-knit tribe of assassins and mercenaries. They answered to the elfin queen, but barely. Ninjas had nothing on this group. Someone wanted you dead and a shadow elf was on the case, the best you could do is buy a really nice life insurance policy for your survivors, because you didn't stand a chance.

I stared at my hand, "So what do Shadow Elves, us, and a vampire warehouse all have in common?"

"Uncle Ulrich," Killian and I said in unison.

"Jinx."

Killian looked at me mystified.

"Now you give me your beer and you can order yourself a Coke."

Sister Magdalena shook her head at me,

"That's not exactly how it's played..."

"It's close enough," I said as I pulled Killian's drink over.

"This is supposed to be fun...?" he asked half-heartedly as he waved the waitress over.

I raised my glass to Father Killarney, but he was too busy chugging down his pint like a frat boy in a shotgunning contest.

"Hey! Hey! Slow down, Father. I'm putting this meal on my AmEx and my credit limit isn't that high."

The old priest wiped off his lips with the back of his hand and set down his glass with resolute finality, "I told you I would tell you about your uncle, so it's time you heard the truth and all of it."

It was not exactly the turn in the conversation I had expected after telling the guy not to run up my bar tab, but shoot, whatever worked. Killian and I leaned forward in unison, a regular set of Frick and Frack.

"Your uncle and your father were two of the finest boys I've ever known. I knew them since they were knee high to a potato." He ran his finger aside his nose like he was Paul Fucking Newman and this was some big secret that now made us a part of his special club, "I didn't always live on this side of the border, you know. I baptized those boys. Oh, they were full of mischief. Exactly how two boys should be. Completely devoted to their duties and their ma, though.

"Then came the day that their gifts woke. I had always suspected, but didn't want to say anything. Your father had more talent than Ulrich. It's a hard thing for a first born to be outstripped by the second. Ulrich started to think if he just worked hard enough, he could make himself a match for your father on the playing field."

Father Killarney leaned back, lost in memories, "And sure enough, he almost did. Unfortunately, rather than learning the skills from the light, someone planted a bug in your uncle's ear about the dark magic. Told him he could have all the power he could want, it wouldn't take much work at all. He just had to make peace with spilling a bit of blood. They started him off easy enough, killing things mercifully, but that monster grew. Pretty soon he was thinking it would be all right to kill people, and kill them in ways not fit for your worst enemy.

"Your uncle had decided humans had no more soul than a rabbit or a cow. It made the killing easier. When your father realized what he was doing, it was the end. Your father hoped that maybe someday your uncle would come back to us, but then your father fell in love with your mother. Oh, that made Ulrich angry. Your uncle felt it was akin to marrying a goat. He crossed over to wipe your ma from the face of God's green Earth."

Father Killarney stared into the bottom of his empty pint, "Fortunately, your uncle couldn't make portals from this world back to the Other Side. He didn't have the inner power. And your father had enough clout to ban Ulrich from the legal portals. So, he was trapped. Your father hoped to keep him here long enough for his head to cool, but then your uncle disappeared and there was no finding him. Your father always believed he must have traveled east, to places where they have maintained the studies of magic and mysticism."

I pulled out the little baggie with the bracelet I lifted off of the ghoul.

"Could he have been working on this?" I asked.

Father Killarney let out a low whistle.

"Well, that's definitely not a tool for the Lord's work," remarked Sister Magdalena dryly.

Father Killarney picked up the baggie with the tine of his fork, holding it out like a stinky polecat skin, "No, he was most definitely not working on this. Dear child, you'd best to be getting rid of this unholy charm as fast as humanly possible."

"Why? What does it do?"

"It is an old magic from the Other Side," Sister Magdalena explained, "It lets the evil undead walk in sunshine."

"Wait, you're telling me that if some nasty gets around to wearing this, the world's olly- olly-oxen-free is offline?"

"I am afraid with this bracelet, there are no longer any timeouts," said Father Killarney. "It isn't so strong that they can do much, but they can walk in the shaded sun nonetheless."

"It has your family crest," Sister Magdalena said as she eyed it cautiously, but then reassured me, "Don't worry. He can't make more. This is one of the most complicated spells ever rumored to exist. It is legendary, really. In fact, everyone thought the spells to create it had been lost. Surprise."

"Your uncle must have brought the bracelet with him when he first came to Earth," said Father Killarney. "There isn't enough magic to do it here, thank God. So unless your uncle can cross, he can't make more."

"Well, there's another reason the vampires might like to give him a hand," I said, hoping there weren't too many of these lovely little trinkets floating around.

The waitress showed up and placed our baskets of food on the table. I reached over for the catsup, and then changed my mind. I didn't need any more oozing red liquids in my life right now. I grabbed the vinegar instead and sprinkled it generously on my fries. I chewed thoughtfully, the potatoes sticking a little in my throat, "I just don't get it, though. If my uncle has had these bracelets since he got trapped here, why did he hold onto them? Why share this particular little bit of magic now?"

"Those vampires must have something he wants very badly."

I shoved a fry in my mouth to squash down the sinking feeling in the pit of my stomach.

"The thing he wants..." I began.

"...is to get to the other side," Father Killarney and I said in unison.

"Jinx," I said, waving to the waitress, "This man is buying me a beer."

"Now, the price of that pint comes out of the collection plate, you know. I took a vow of poverty."

"I'm sure you can expense it from the service fee you're going to invoice me," I said as I took the icy glass from the waitress. "So the vampires want my uncle on the Other Side so that he can make more of these creepy little fashion accessories and Ulrich wants to get over to the Other Side because he misses killing my family..." I sipped thoughtfully, "So, some vampires came and visited me last night---"

Father Killarney just about came over the table at me to check my neck.

"Don't worry! I had backup," I said, trying to calm him down.

"What are you doing talking to vampires, Maggie?" Father Killarney hissed, making me feel like a sixteen-year old kid who had gotten her first speeding ticket.

"I didn't WANT to," I insisted lamely. "They said they were trying to save the world."

"You know better than that," Father Killarney chided.

"I kept the crossbow on them the entire time," reassured Killian.

"They said that there is a new master who is trying to tear down the boundary and they warned me I needed to find a jade lion," I added. "We think it's what the Shadow Elves picked up in the warehouse."

Father Killarney leaned back in his seat with disapproval in his voice, "Never heard of such a thing."

"Well, whether you've heard of it or not, it appears to be real," I said. I pushed the rest of my fries onto his plate, "I need your help."

He eyed the fries, trying to decide whether to stay miffed at me for consorting with the enemy, which I feel should be noted that I only did for the survival of the human race, or surrender to the comforts of my salty, fried peace offering. Peace won.

Killian passed him the malt vinegar.

"If you need help with the Northern magic, I'm better than anyone else you'll find on this side of the pond. But a jade lion..." Father Killarney rubbed his whiskers thoughtfully, "Jade is an eastern material. Lions are guardians, for sure. I've got a friend in Chinatown, his name is Xiaoming. He might know..."

"We should pay him a visit," said Killian and I in unison.

"Waitress, the next round is on this guy," I called out.

Chapter 25

Old Chinatown is a fun place. It was originally built as a shopping area by the local Asian population. Nowadays, the cobblestone courtyard and little trinket shops serve as a smoke screen for secret Mahjong halls and borderline sweat shops.

We walked down a particularly stinky alley to a tiny, little doorway squeezed tightly between two buildings. The red security gate had some newspaper stuffed in the lock and opened with a gentle push. We walked up the concrete steps to a landing where dusty California succulents sat baking next to two dog-sized lion guards.

I knocked on the aluminum screen door and could hear shuffling feet inside.

When the door opened, I met the eyes of a bitty old man, cigarette burning in the corner of his mouth.

"Xiaoming?"

His sunken chest sported a stained wife-beater and his blue striped boxer shorts had seen better days. You could tell he had dressed up for company, though, because he had managed to throw on a ratty old robe and open-toed slippers to show off his holey socks.

"Come in," he demanded. "Take off your shoes. You get the dirt in here."

He appeared to have one vocal level and that was shouting on the same note.

I introduced myself, "Father Killarney said you might be able to help us."

Xiaoming sat down at the kitchen table and pounded his thighs. The room was filled with sweetly scented incense that made a migraine sufferer out of me. I blinked back the headache and came over, stooping beneath the beaded curtain dividing the kitchen from his sparse living room. Killian was busy looking at an altar over in the corner.

"Don't touch that, elf!" shouted our host. "You mess up everything!"

Killian backed away, "My apologies."

"You just a big fat elf with your big fat elf fingers. You sit here."

He pounded on the seat beside him. Killian dutifully came over, realizing he was no match for this guy.

I pulled out a piece of paper with the sketch

on it, deciding permanent Sharpie was probably a bit safer than trying to maintain the drawing through hand washings.

"We were tracking an object…"

"This bad," Xiaoming stated.

"What?"

"This is bad symbol. What you tracking?"

"A jade lion."

Xiaoming took a long drag on his cigarette and stared me in the eye.

"Do you know anything about it?" I asked.

"Jade lion cannot leave Other Side. Where you take it?"

"I didn't take it anywhere!" I protested.

"This elf symbol. You, stinking elf, where you take it?"

Killian leaned forward, "On my family's honor, we had no knowledge of this theft. This fair lady and I, we wish to restore it to its proper place. But we do not know who stole it or what it even is."

"You get it back!" Xiaoming barked. "I tell you where it go."

I gave him a sideways glance, "If you weren't a friend of Father Killarney, I'd like to tell *you* where to go."

He glared back at me, "I the only one who know the truth of jade lion."

"Obviously not the only one. We've got

vampires and elves and really shitty extended family after it, too."

Xiaoming took out his cigarette and pointed a leathery finger at the symbol, "This from Shadow Elf. They not know meaning of jade lion. They only know it thing of power. You say vampire after it?"

"Yes."

"And 'shitty family'? They after it, too?"

"Yes."

"Why you after it?"

I sighed and pointed my thumb at Killian, "Because this elf here hired me to keep the border between Earth and the Other Side from collapsing and, evidently, this little jade lion is something important."

Xiaoming nodded, "That is a good reason."

He took a drag off his cigarette and sized me up, "Okay, friend of Father Killarney, I will tell you." He leaned forward, "This jade lion very old. It comes from China. You know where China is?"

"I am not an idiot, Xiaoming."

"Educational system in America is not as good as in China. You may be idiot. It is hard to tell with you white people."

The elf started to laugh and tried to cover it up as a cough into his sleeve. I elbowed him in the ribs.

"Xiaoming, I've got to figure out if I'm hanging with my sister tonight or if I've got time to make it back to the portal. Let's speed through the insults and get to the info part of this conversation."

"This jade lion protect the Other Side portal to China. It was made by emperor who was a very powerful man. Very strong. Even when old, he does not need dried tiger penis to make the babies."

"Whoa! Whoa! Whoa! Too much information, Xiaoming."

"That is how strong emperor is! He have many Shaolin monks to carve this jade lion with their bare hands."

"You can't carve jade---"

He cut me off and stared me dead in the eye to make sure I understood the gravity of the claim he was making, "This emperor so powerful, his monks so powerful, they carve jade with their fingernails."

Alrighty. Jade lion. Carved out of Shaolin monk fingernails. As awful as it sounds to say, I'd heard of stranger things. I motioned for him to continue

"He make two lions of strongest elements. One jade. One diamond. They can open or close portal. Jade Lion on Other Side facing Earth. Diamond Lion on Earth facing Other Side. If facing wrong way, portal closed. Facing right way, portal opened. Anyone can make portal. He make it for his son who is not magic."

Little lights started coming on in my head, "Wait. You're saying that if you have someone on either side of the boundary with control of these lions, you can just tear right through, no problem?"

"That, white girl, is what I am saying to you. You say the Jade Lion taken by the Shadow Elves? That is better than vampire, but still, not good. You say shitty relatives after it, too. This is bad. You, elf, you get jade lion from Shadow Elves and make safe on Other Side. You, white girl, you get diamond lion."

"Where is the diamond lion?" I asked.

"I do not know. Somewhere on Earth. Lions cannot cross boundary. He is here on Earth somewhere. You find diamond lion and bring him to me. I take him to China and keep him safe."

"How can you keep the diamond lion safe? Your security gate doesn't even shut."

And then there was a growl from the door. I looked over and the two concrete lions had turned to stare at me in a very non-concrete manner. One of them lifted up his lip to give me a low growl.

My bad.

"Xiaoming, you can't blame a girl for being nervous about your security when you failed to mention your statuary comes to life."

He waved at the lions and they returned to their original positions.

"You bring it to me. I take it back to China. I have a passport. You find the diamond lion. And you tell Father Killarney he owe me money from our last poker game."

"I will certainly tell him that."

And with that, Xiaoming waved us out. Killian and I rose from our seats and backed out of the room feeling a bit like we had been steamrolled.

Chapter 26

I clicked the little doohickey on my keychain and my car merrily beeped at me. I let out a groan as I saw that there was a parking ticket sitting on my windshield. Why is it every time I try to save a buck and park at a meter instead of the garage, I end up having to pay $40?

I leaned over and shoved the ticket in my purse.

"What's that?" asked Killian.

"Just a donation request to support the brave public servants of Los Angeles during this time of budgetary shortfalls."

In the Other Side, they knew me well enough to let it slide. Note to self: get snuggly with local law enforcement. Or just the meter maids.

I revved up the car and looked in my rear view window, noticing a navy blue SUV pulling out. I waited for it to go around, but the driver waved me to cut in front of him. Evidently, there were such things as gentlemen in Los Angeles.

A couple miles down the road though, I

realized that the SUV was following me turn for turn. I slowly wove around the blocks and side streets until we were back by Xiaoming's. The SUV stuck two cars behind me the whole way.

"Hey, Killian?"

"Yes?" he said as he flipped through my CD collection. The man had trouble sitting still.

"Look in the rear view. You recognize that blue SUV?"

Killian readjusted my mirror so that he could get a good look without having to turn around, "No."

The driver was completely non-descript. White guy, brown hair, sunglasses. I'd have trouble picking him out of a lineup.

"Thoughts?" I asked.

"Outrun him?"

I looked at the wall-to-wall car bumpers and their red flashy brake lights in front of us as far as the eye could see.

"Let's try Plan B."

I pulled over to an empty space and turned off the engine. I saw the blue SUV scramble and pull up at a red curb. Amateur.

"Stay," I commanded Killian. And he did. If only commanding human men was usually as easy...

I got out of the car and walked back to the SUV. The guy tried to turn on his engine and pull out, but I decided to stand in his way.

I knocked on his window and he rolled it down.

"Can I help you?" I asked.

"I'm just an ordinary citizen. You should get out of the street before a hazardous situation unfolds," he stammered.

I folded my arms and leaned on his windowsill, giving him a good ol' look down my shirt. He gulped uncomfortably.

"Now, don't be like that," I smiled. "I caught your tail fair and square. Now, why don't you tell me what I can do for you?"

"I... uh... I thought... Want to go out on a date?" he offered lamely.

"Listen, I'm asking really nicely," I said as I reached into the car and grabbed him by both lapels. "You seem like you're new to all this and stuff. Why don't you just tell me why you're following me and I won't reshape your nose into something with a bit more character."

He sighed and pulled out a badge, "We received a tip that an international smuggler of rare antiquities resided in that building and that we should monitor it. I saw you go in and come out, but I did not see an exchange take place so... I thought maybe I should follow you."

I smoothed out the guy's shirt, "Agent...?"

"Agent Hogs."

"Wait, really?"

He blushed bright red, "It was a thing at Ellis Island when my family came over…"

I was getting sidetracked, "Listen, Agent Hogs, I am not a member of an international smuggling ring, nor is the man who resides there. Xiaoming is an historian and a scholar. That's it. Whoever gave you this information was lying."

Agent Hogs protested, "He has a whole lot of trips to China…"

I pulled out my business card and handed it to him, "He deals in antiquities, Agent Hogs. He doesn't steal."

At least I hoped that Xiaoming didn't steal, but the agent looked utterly defeated, so rock on with my bad self for hitting a plausible truth with a shot in the dark.

"We have reason to believe that Xiaoming's safety may be at risk," I continued, trying to assure the rookie. "You staking out his house is probably a great idea. Just let me know if there is any trouble or if any suspicious characters go to visit, okay?"

"Okay."

"It was a pleasure meeting you, Agent."

"Likewise."

I walked back to my car and watched as Agent Hogs pulled out a cell phone before driving down the street. I opened the door and climbed inside, "Well, that's handled. Let's find ourselves a diamond lion statue."

Unfortunately, the search was momentarily delayed as my car and the cars around me were thrown thirty feet.

Chapter 27

Car alarms were going off and sirens could be heard in the distance.

"That fucking boundary..." I swore, holding my hand to my temple. My forehead was bleeding where I had conked myself on the suicide bar. "Why is it that my airbags never deploy?"

Killian was on the alert, looking where the boundary had bulged. It shimmered for just a moment and then went back to normal.

"Another failed portal," he said.

"Yah, that's what I was thinking," I muttered as I looked around at the chaos. Stunned civilians were starting to get out of their cars and exchange insurance information with one another. I got out to see how bad the damage was to my vehicle. I sighed as I eyed the dented-in door, thinking about all the fun new claims I was going to have to explain to my insurance company.

"I've never felt such an earthquake!" remarked a pale, redheaded gal in a car one over.

Other than the cosmetic damage, it appeared that my car hadn't hit anyone, so I was getting ready to hop back inside when I felt a hand grab my elbow.

I turned, ready to nail whoever it was in the face, but pulled my punch when I saw it was Xiaoming.

"Xiaoming? What are you doing here?" I asked.

"I followed SUV following you. Make sure you not big, fat liar. You not liar. You stupid. You come now!"

There was another terrible bulge in the boundary. It sent a VW bug through a live animals market and hundreds of chickens were suddenly flying free. Score one for the chickens.

"That is Jade Lion," said Xiaoming. "Too much power. Only works with world walker. Cannot work in hands of non-magic without Diamond Lion. But if lion rests eyes on you, border will open. You will be a noodle and the border will be like mouth." He made a slurping motion, indicating what fun I had in store if I happened to face the wrong way. I needed to train this guy in the fine art of conversation. Ew.

"You must follow me."

We ducked into a smoky mahjong hall. It was kind of like a church bingo place, long folding brown tables and chairs. They obviously hadn't gotten the notice on the "no indoor smoking" ban. Old guys chewed on black cigarettes and stared at us suspiciously. Xiaoming spat out something in Chinese and hustled us through. I saw a group pick up their table and stand at the ready to place it in front of our exit spot.

We dashed through the concrete plaza of old Chinatown, past the brightly colored buildings and a statue of some random Chinese leader.

Xiaoming led us over to the subway. He shooed us up to the elevated platform, "I will bring your car to Father Killarney. You go to top of train station and wait for me."

Chapter 28

I wasn't too sure how great I felt about hanging out on an elevated platform to catch a train instead of staying nice and safe with my feet on the ground. But for whatever reason, Xiaoming thought we needed to take the train. So be it.

After about ten minutes watching clouds of smoke erupt all over Chinatown from whatever amateur was trying to wield the lion, I looked down the track for the train.

And then I saw our transport.

If I wouldn't have felt so completely ridiculous doing it, I would have rubbed my eyes in disbelief. There was Xiaoming, cigarette hanging out of the corner of his mouth, on a pump cart like you see in the old Wile E. Coyote cartoons. The thing that made this cart different was that the whole thing was made of polished silver.

I stuck my thumb out and Xiaoming pulled up to the platform.

"Nice ride," I remarked.

"I pimped it for you," he replied dryly.

I always get the comedians.

Killian leapt over to the cart and then held out his hand for me. Usually, I would scoff at such niceties, but my head was bleeding fairly profusely in that way that only head wounds can bleed.

"Thanks," I said. He helped me to sit and then took a place on the opposite handle. Between him and Xiaoming, we accelerated to a pretty respectable speed.

"So," I said, trying to come up with some polite chit chat, "you just keep this baby locked in your garage?"

Xiaoming grunted, "It is for protection. Silver wheels keep us from bad magic attack. Like your stealth bomber, but on train track."

Stealth. Right. You know, if you're not blind to three people perched on a shiny handcart and deaf to rhythmic squeaky pumping.

"So, where are we off to?" I asked, my eyes watching the buildings as they whizzed by.

"I get you out of Chinatown before you destroy it."

"Excuse me, I did not destroy anything."

"You bring fist of destruction. You will not make portal in my neighborhood."

"I am the victim here!" I pointed out, holding up my blood-covered hand.

"Does not matter who started it. I end it. You

go home."

"Killian is the one that got me into this. I wouldn't even be here if it wasn't for him. If you want to blame someone, maybe you should bark up that tree."

Xiaoming gave Killian the old fisheye and then declared, "He working. You sitting. He okay. You lazy."

There was no winning with this guy. He and Father Killarney were a match made in heaven.

"How they find you so fast?" Xiaoming scowled at me.

"I have no idea," I replied, "Although you need to be on the lookout. Evidently, your place is being..."

I'm an idiot.

That tail had nothing to do with the long arm of the law. There was no antiquities stakeout. I was a chump and had even given the guy my contact information.

"Crap," I said.

"What you do now?" Xiaoming accused.

I looked over at Killian apologetically, "The guy in the SUV who was tailing us. He looked like a fed. I had a little talk with him. Thought I was doing you a favor by straightening him out. The attack came right after he made a positive ID on me."

"You so stupid."

"Yah, Xiaoming, I get that," I snapped. God, he was like a high school gym teacher from hell who kept telling the fat kid all she had to do was run faster. I turned to Killian, "I can't believe I didn't pick up on it."

Xiaoming gave a huff, "You able to open portal. Lion is like a positive magnet and you a negative magnet. It drawn to you. They just have to find where you are and point. You like diamond lion, except not as good."

"Thanks for the kind words, Xiaoming. Have you ever considered a career in motivational speaking?"

"There are ways to talk between border. You say you have 'shitty' family here on Earth, correct?"

"And some very nice family, too, I'll have you know."

"Your phone go through border so you can talk to family?"

I thought only my dad was strong enough to set up an inter-dimensional phone line. Evidently I was wrong, "So the fake fed has a phone line to the Other Side, too, and told them where to aim the Jade Lion?"

"If you facing right way, jade lion open up portal like jian sword to enemy belly button. You make sure not to look at border when it is coming at you."

I finally got what he was trying to tell me. Facing the right way at the wrong time was hazardous for my health. I couldn't believe we had survived this long, "Killian? Did you know I wasn't supposed to be looking at the border?"

"Not in inkling."

Seriously, if fate was going to suck me into an alternate dimension because of an inappropriate glance, I didn't really think I had much of a fighting chance.

"Okay. Well. You just promise you'll spin me like we're playing Pin the Tail on the Wood Sprite the next time they try to punch a hole through."

We entered a tunnel and the red tip of Xiaoming's cigarette was the only light in the place. Thank god the guy could chain smoke like a mutha otherwise we would have been plunged into complete darkness. Still, as he lit up his fourth, hacking up a nasty wad of phlegm, I commented, "You don't worry much about your health, do you?"

"I read air quality report," he said, removing the cigarette from his mouth to point it at me, "At least I have filter."

As we emerged from the tunnel, a familiar brownie was standing at the switch. Pipistrelle threw the lever and we rolled off onto a side track.

"Pipistrelle! You found us!" I said with a smile. I know he had been pretty much useless up until this point, but I was sort of warming up to him like you do a friend's puppy.

The little guy gave a smart salute.

"My master sent me with word of your uncle," he informed us cheerily.

"What?" I asked as Killian and I hopped off the cart.

"Ulrich is coming to kill you," said the brownie.

I looked up at Xiaoming. He gave me a "so it goes" sort of shrug, flipped a couple gears on the handcar, and took off the way he came, leaving us standing out there in that field.

Good to know he cared.

"Pipistrelle, do you know when or how?" I asked as I patted myself down to make sure my stake was still within easy reach.

The brownie nodded so hard he almost fell over, "I learned that he has brought a clan of vampires over by way of a sulfur circle. They will come tonight. You would do well to find shelter before the sun gives way to the darkness."

He was so excited to be able to give us something useful, he made the imminent attack by a clan of vampires sound like it was a surprise party.

I looked over at the hill. The sun had already

touched its ridge, "Killian, we gotta get moving. We've got a half hour, maybe forty five minutes."

"Pipistrelle," Killian said patiently, crouching down so that he was almost eye level, "are they tracking us?"

"They do not know where you are currently. I heard him say that you had visited Chinatown. They will most likely smell you there and come find you here."

Killian looked up at me worried.

I calmed him, "The handcar's silver wheels will have protected our path."

Killian pointed at my head wound, "Except that you are bleeding."

Fucking elf. He was right. I had probably dribbled enough blood along the way for a pack of regular old hound dogs to sniff us out, much less a gaggle of blood suckers who track bodily fluids for a living.

"Let's just worry about them tracking us from this point forward. It'll be pure luck if they find us all the way out here."

Killian became very still, "Do you think they know about your sister?"

Shit.

Her house was a fortress, but other than that, my sister was utterly defenseless. Her husband was a great guy, but he knew more about battling it out with the vampires of Wall Street than the more garden-variety blood sucking ones. It appears I may have inadvertently brought an (un)living nightmare to her doorstep and I was all the way across town.

"We can't go there tonight," I said. "Not while they are tracking me. They shouldn't know about Mindy, but we can't go back there again until this is done."

I turned to the little brownie, "Pipistrelle, as soon as we are safe for the night, I need you to go take care of my sister. Get your boss to put a glamour around her and her husband. He owes us one more mark and I'm calling it in. He has to protect them from anyone who would do them harm."

Pipistrelle nodded seriously, "I hear and I will obey. My master will protect Maggie's sister and Maggie's sister's husband. I will make sure!"

I ruffled that little guy's hair and he looked like he was about to pop from the show of affection.

I turned back to Killian, "If we find a payphone, I'll call her and give her the rundown."

Killian pointed to my cell phone, "Do you want to try to call her now?"

I thought about that damned business card I had just handed over to the faux government goon, "They'll trace any number I dial, or at least that's what I'd do."

Killian nodded in understanding, "Well, then, it appears we are on our own tonight. Pipistrelle? Do you have any recommendations for shelter?"

The little guy nodded, "There is an inn close by."

Killian turned to me, "Do we risk harming innocent people by staying there?"

It was probably a deep philosophical question, but I was still bleeding, "As long as we get ourselves over a threshold and nobody around us invites any of the bastards in, everyone should be okay. They can only hold us under siege until morning."

"Unless they have your uncle's talisman."

"Right."

Next time I saw my uncle, I was going to let him know he was a real jerk.

Killian held out his arm in a sweeping bow to the brownie, "To the inn, Pipistrelle!"

Twilight began to fall and every squirrel in the brush sounded like an attack. Fortunately, you can't go too far in LA without running into civilization somewhere. The desert-like scrub gave way to urban blight and old homes. There were streets and buckled sidewalks which made moving much easier. The thing about Los Angeles, though, is that no one walks. You can go for miles and miles and see plenty of cars, but not a single soul. To say it is creepy is an understatement, especially when you're waiting for a clan of vampires to jump out at you at any moment.

As the darkness closed in, we started hugging the buildings and checking around the corners before we moved. My heart rate was definitely up and my senses on high alert.

The last light of day faded to nothing and Killian picked up his pace to a brisk jog. Besides elves being absolutely gorgeous, they're pretty much crazy athletes and have never heard of "fatigue" or "dropping dead from exhaustion".

Trying to keep up with the fairy version of Carl Lewis meant that I almost didn't see the vampire. He was hiding behind the column of an old, abandoned gas station as we ran by. His pale face matched the peeling paint of the building.

The vamp tried to slink away. I realized I was running at him as if heading straight towards the undead was an automatic default setting in my primal lizard brain. If I let the sucker get away, he'd tell his buddies, and Killian and I were toast.

Killian almost didn't notice that I had turned off. He glanced over his shoulder and then stopped as he saw me charge towards the abandoned building.

"Maggie?" he called in a worried voice.

I pulled out my silver stake and broke into a

flat out sprint. The vamp was having a tough time navigating the steep slope behind the building. Tough as in "still supernaturally strong and faster than any person could ever be", but not as quick as a vampire might like. The fact he was struggling meant he was a young one and perhaps his brains were not, shall we say, the most oxygen-rich bag in the blood bank.

I had one shot. His back was to me, he was halfway up the hill. I aimed and threw. It was a long shot to expect it to A) hit him and B) pierce his heart. But that's what happened and I was totally impressed with myself. The vamp went down and he was out.

I looked over at Killian and Pipistrelle.

"Did you see that?" I said, pointing at the pile of ex-vampire.

The little brownie gave me a thumbs up.

I climbed up the hill to go retrieve my stake.

Killian hissed at me, "Get back here! We have to go!"

I glanced over my shoulder, "It's fine. I just need to get my stake. It'll be awhile before they figure out where to come looking for him."

Evidently not long enough, though, because the moment I turned back, there was another undead mug peeking over the hill at me.

Crap.

They must have just sent out pairs in a huge wide net hoping that one of them would get lucky. And unfortunately for us, today was their lucky day.

I grabbed the stake and wiped it on my pants, "You're right. I'm wrong. Let's go. Now."

I skittered down the hill. I knew when to fight and when to run away to fight again another day. Or when to run in the hopes of not having to fight at all.

"What did you see?" asked Killian, catching up with me as I tore off down the street.

"Another scout. I don't know if they were trying to taunt me into following them right into a trap or if they have a buddy system now, but whatever it is, it is bad and we need to get out of here."

Killian didn't need another warning.

We turned, following Pipistrelle down a residential street. He seemed to think this was a great evening jaunt and tons of fun.

"Pipistrelle, quit humming!" I hissed for the umpteenth time.

He shut up, but I could tell the musical earworm was still singing itself in his head, because every now and again, he'd pause to bust a move.

I guess brownies aren't too concerned about being turned into vampire food.

We turned another street and there was the most blessed sight I had ever seen - a great big yellow hotel sign of a dive not even good enough to sail under a corporate flag. The neon light read "vacancy".

I'm sure that Killian and I looked like hell when we came in, but the guy behind the bulletproof glass looked like he had seen worse.

"One room or two?" he asked, barely looking up from his game of minesweeper.

"One," we said in unison.

"With two beds," I added.

The guy handed us two actual, real keys on green plastic key chains. As we were leaving, I turned back and said offhanded, "Thanks. Don't invite any vampires in."

The guy behind the glass gave me a sarcastic smile and went back to his game. Boy, I hope he listened.

Pipistrelle had disappeared by the time we got outside. I hoped the little dude was on his way to my sister's and/or was hiding somewhere safe. I didn't need a tiny corpse on my guilt list.

Our room was a threadbare, nasty flea trap. The carpet was a throw-up green and the walnut laminate furniture chipped and covered in a greasy film. I hated to think of the action the bedspreads had seen.

And yet, I have to say as I crossed its threshold, it was one of the most beautiful rooms I had ever laid eyes on.

We got in, threw the deadbolt, and turned off the light so that we could watch the street.

I could see the vampires stake out the place, so to speak.

"How many?" asked Killian, peeking over my shoulder.

"I counted five. I don't know how many more we can't see."

I let the blinds close and walked over to the bed to pull off my shoes.

Killian lay across the other bed and picked up the remote control, flipping it to The Discovery Channel. Mike Rowe, had I got a dirty job suggestion for you...

The hours faded one into the other. There were knocks at the door and knocks at the window, announcements of pizza we didn't order and taunts to come out. Killian just turned up the volume.

Around 2:00AM, I started hitting the wall as the vamps continued to hound us. The fact the night manager hadn't called the police led me to believe he hadn't heeded my warning and was probably sporting a couple of nasty hickeys. We were well into a QVC wasteland of late night commercials. I was moments away from believing that a food vacuum sealer held all the keys to happiness in a re-sealable plastic bag when a heavy thunk caused the door to shake on its hinges.

I looked over at Killian, "I swear to god if they don't cut it out with all the banging, I'm going to go out there and kill them all."

"I would be happy to carry your extra gun," Killian replied.

I sighed as I flipped stations.

"So what is the plan for tomorrow?" Killian asked.

I had no idea, "I need to go reclaim my car from Father Killarney. Maybe he'll have some ideas."

"Do you feel like we have missed something?" Killian mused.

I kept flipping stations, "Nah, there's really nothing good on."

"I meant about the vampires."

He got out a pad and pen from the bedside drawer and started mapping out his thoughts à la pictogram. I folded up the pillow beneath my head and looked over at what he was trying to flowchart.

"They want to walk in the sun, which your uncle is working on," Killian said. "He wants to return home, and the vampires are gathering up the lions. They had the jade lion, but they don't seem to have the diamond lion, yet. Why bother themselves with you?"

The pieces of the puzzle fell into place.

I took the pen out of his hand and drew a little stick figure with straight black hair and eyelashes holding an ugly kitty cat, "They think I have it."

Killian looked me dead in the eye, having the same moment of realization. He threw himself back on his pillow and stared at the ceiling, "Well, at least the solution is easy."

"And what is that?"

Mirrored grins crossed our faces.

"Get the diamond lion first," Killian and I said at the same time.

"Jinx," said Killian. We stared at one another in silence before he asked, "Now what?"

"I'm not allowed to talk until I buy you a Coke," I replied.

"Seems like a fair exchange."

I threw the pillow at his head.

He caught it and put it on the far side of his bed before taking the remote out of my hands and turning off the light, "Rest. I promise to wake you in two hours time or prior to Armageddon, whichever comes first."

You don't get into my line of work if you don't learn how to grab sleep whenever it comes. Sure, the ground was probably more comfortable than the beds we were on and death was literally at our door, but I sandwiched my ears between my remaining pillows and was out.

I woke up with dawn breaking in the room. Killian had opened up the blinds and was looking outside.

"You were going to wake me," I said, feeling like a total slacker.

Killian shrugged, "For some reason, they all took off and I fell asleep shortly after you."

So much for him having the first watch.

I joined him over at the window. The vamps were definitely gone and the sun was definitely up.

"What shall we do today?" Killian asked.

"I say we check out and find some food," I replied, looking down at the office, "I'm thinking continental breakfast might not be offered this morning."

To our surprise, the night manager was still sitting there, still playing his computer games. The office all around him looked spic and span, though. Pipistrelle probably got bored and decided to do some cleaning while the guy wasn't looking.

The night manager was completely underwhelmed that we were checking out.

"Some friends of yours stopped by," he said. "We don't allow unregistered guests in the rooms."

"We did not let them in," I replied in earnestness.

"Good," he said, sliding the receipt towards me.

I raised an eyebrow at the bill and noted to Killian, "I'm adding this to your tab and expect to be reimbursed."

The night clerk threw me the ol' fisheye.

"I'm doing a job for him..." I protested.

"Not interested in knowing what kind of 'job' you did for him last night. If the cops come, I don't want any information. Don't come back. Got it?"

Fantastic. I was sitting there saving the world from destruction, and this jerk off thought I was hooking in his hotel.

I scrawled out my signature sloppily on the receipt and stalked out of the lobby. I didn't even look back as Killian jogged over to keep up.

"You could have protected my honor," I sulked.

"The lady doth protest too much," he replied.

"Um, excuse me. The guy was thinking I was whoring myself out at a $49.99 motel. You could have set the record straight."

"It is a better cover than 'I am a tracker and I am hiding out from vampires'," Killian replied.

Why did that fucking elf always have to be right?

Chapter 29

We grabbed breakfast in a greasy spoon place that featured a flickering neon "Open" sign and a sparsely populated parking lot. Their cleaning crew appeared to be of the same ilk of the folks taking care of the motel, but their coffee was good and they spared no butter on their eggs, which is all I ever really ask for in life. After that, we hiked over to the train and took it to Hollywood and Highland, the heart of the entertainment capital of the world.

I feel so bad for all the tourists that come out to Hollywood expecting to see glam and glitter. It isn't really the heart anymore. More like the appendix. Sort of smelly and useless and should probably be cut out sometime soon. Most of the studios migrated over to the Valley because of space and all that is really left of Hollywood are some handprints in the cement and some dirty stars in the sidewalk. Some big corporations had made noises years ago that they were going to come clean up the city, but ten years later, all we got was a dumb shopping mall and some chain stores no one went to because the parking was so lousy.

The one cool thing that Hollywood has, though, is its subway stations. The one we exited out of has old movie projector reels hung like acoustic tiles from the ceiling. The gorgeous art didn't increase ridership, but it made for some pretty viewing for those willing to hazard traveling underground in earthquake territory.

Father Killarney's parish was over on Sunset. It is a nice little place with a healthy attendance of upstanding citizens.

The door to the church was unlocked when we got there. I opened it up and he was on the altar explaining to a young family the ins and outs of the baptism ceremony.

He acknowledged me by jerking his head towards the rectory.

Killian and I made our way into the back room. The red carpet was almost as thick as the ancient layers of lead-based white paint on the walls.

There were a couple of chairs and a refrigerator where the sacramental wine was kept. I knew from history there would also be some soda and bottles of water.

I grabbed some refreshments for Killian and

myself while we waited.

You would think that in a church, you'd be safe from the creepy crawlies, but evidently not.

I felt them before I saw them. It was like a surge of electricity up my back that made the hairs on my arms stand on end. That little zing is what makes me such a good tracker.

I was on my feet with my daggers in hand before Killian even had a chance to finish swallowing.

I ran over to the sanctuary and flung open the door.

There were four ghouls walking down the aisle. I was guessing it wasn't to exchange marital vows.

"Father Killarney!" I called, trying to keep my voice as calm as possible so as not to alert the very nice family with the very nice baby they were about to become lunch for some undead, shape-shifting zombies. "Father Killarney, I am afraid that your next appointment has arrived. I'd be happy to see to them. Perhaps you would like to take this family to your office."

Father Killarney gave the invading party a glance. He started to greet the ghouls with a friendly, "Why, good afternoon Jerry and---"

So evidently the ghouls were able to cross the holy threshold by assuming the shapes of exparishioners, tricky ghouls. But Father Killarney was no fool. His eyes followed the four limping fellows, who were looking a little worse for wear and definitely in need of a corpse sandwich in order to keep their girlish figures, and did the math.

Father Killarney turned to the family, "I apologize. I had forgotten the church is being used for a film shoot this afternoon." He turned to the ghouls and shouted good-naturedly, "My compliments to the special effects department."

He turned back to the family and their tiny little bundle of joy and ushered them towards the exit, "Right this way. If you'll follow me to the rectory, there is just a little paperwork that needs to be completed."

He grabbed a crucifix-on-a-stick on his way out. It is such a multi-purpose kind of religious symbol. It can be carried up in the processional to start a mass and can also be used to brain bad guys.

As he passed me, he whispered, "Get those ghouls out of my church before I have to re-hallow this ground."

"Aye aye, captain," I said.

The moment the door closed, Killian's collapsible staff was uncollapsed and out in his hands. He started swinging it in slow even circles before him.

"All warmed up?" I asked. "Wouldn't want you to strain a muscle."

"If I were a baseball player," he replied, "I would say that I am ready to knock the cover off the ball."

The ghoul closest to me hissed like a territorial old tomcat. Oh, he had no idea whose corner he was trying to piss in.

I lifted my knives, "Batter up!"

Downing ghouls is a messy business, but they move pretty slow and aren't particularly bright. The first ghoul went down without a fight. Cut him across the throat, got sprayed by a boatload of goo as he dissolved, and that was that. Killian wasn't having too rough a time with his dude, either. I heard a sound like a watermelon being smashed with a baseball bat and the ghoul was gone.

The other two ghouls turned away fearfully, finally figuring out they had eaten the wrong parishioners at the wrong parish.

Sometimes you gotta teach the forces of darkness a lesson, though, and unfortunately for them, I wasn't feeling particularly "live and let live" at the moment. A simple "my bad" was not gonna get them off the hook.

The ghouls took off in a limping jog towards the exit and Killian and I were right after them.

But as we followed them out the door, I was

halted in my tracks.

There had to be at least thirty ghouls standing on the steps of the church, waiting for us to come out. I had never heard of ghouls organizing, but maybe they ate a union leader and started getting some good ideas.

Making a stand against the undead in front of a church in broad daylight while armed with a concealed gun and a couple knives was not my idea of a good time, but we live in an imperfect world and I wasn't about to let them cross the church's threshold again, even if that meant getting my hair messed up.

But then one of the ghouls moved towards me and I knew this was a much bigger problem than I had originally assessed. That ghoul moved fast. And when it was moving towards me, its eyeballs gave off a weird golden glow and I knew we weren't dealing with the slow shambling undead.

We had an army of doppelgangers on our hands.

Doppelgangers, for the uninitiated, are very smart. And they are very fast. And just to restate, I counted about thirty of them on the steps in broad daylight.

The first one was upon me before I could even warn Killian.

Dead is dead one way or another and

doppelgangers die just the same as other creatures from the Other Side. I fit a knife between the breastbone and the ribs of the first creature that came at me. As it fell, its ghoulish glamour disappeared and the doppelganger faded into shadow.

And then all the doppelgangers decided to play a neat little trick and assume the shapes of Killian and me.

"Killian!" I shouted as a guy who looked like the spitting image of Killian attacked.

"What?" responded eight other Killians. Fantastic. A horde of Mensa monsters.

"I'm only going to fight versions of myself. You only fight versions of yourself, got it?"

Which was, of course, an invitation to every Killian doppelganger to attack me and every Maggie doppelganger to go after Killian. I tried to keep my eyes on him. It wasn't too hard. I knew that whoever was at the center of the mob of Maggie clones was my guy.

The doppelgangers weren't fighting fair and coming at me one at a time, though. It was a free for all brawl and my only goal was not to get stuck at the bottom of the dog pile.

I got a knock to the jaw that had me seeing stars and I'm sure loosened a couple teeth. I was stabbing anything that moved. I could hear some tourists close by comment, "Oh, they must be shooting a movie."

I just wish we had a director somewhere to shout "cut".

My knuckles were bloody and I know for a fact if it wasn't for all the adrenaline, I would have collapsed long ago. I caught a punch to the eye that sent me reeling into the arms of another doppelganger. She tried to hold me down so that the other me could run me through, but I spun her around and felt her catch the knife meant for me.

Enough with the stabbing. Things were starting to get complicated. I could tell that the doppelgangers were starting to lose track over who was who. I pulled out my gun and started firing point blank. I heard the tourists start screaming.

"Just special effects, folks!"

I don't think they believed me.

I felt something crack across the back of my skull. I staggered to the ground and then rolled as quick as I could to my back, kicking with my feet as the doppelganger tried to land on top of me. I raised my gun and fired off a round straight into her heart. The kickback jarred my aching bones. It felt like all my cartilage had disappeared and there was no cushion in my joints. Another gal came at me and I fired again. And another and I squeezed off another shot.

And then all was quiet. I could hear sirens in the distance. I guess the tourists weren't buying my Hollywood bullshit.

All the doppelgangers were gone, but Killian... ah god. Killian was lying prone in a puddle, face dripping with mud and gutter water.

"Crap," I muttered as I drug my aching body over to his. God, it just hurt to move. It was like I had an army of mutant bunny rabbits kicking out a drum beat inside my head. I pushed his shoulder and rolled him over to his back, hoping he hadn't drowned in two inches of liquid. I couldn't feel a pulse and he wasn't breathing.

"Come on, you bastard."

I beat out five paces on his heart and lowered my lips to his. Another five paces. Another two breaths.

He came to life with a gasp like someone had punched him in the stomach, coughing and rolling onto his side.

His eyes were dull, but he was alive.

"I want to get you to a hospital."

"We're on the wrong side," he mumbled.

Fuck him and his green elvish blood.

"We'll go back."

He gripped my arm softly, "I'm fine. We have to find your uncle."

"I'm not having the queen of the elfin empire

knocking at my door at 2AM because I let you talk me out of getting medical attention."

He didn't even give me much of a fight, and that scared me more than all the spooky things we had just fought off.

"Come on, Killian," I said, wrapping my body warm around his. "I'll get you home."

World jumping from an unmarked point to another is idiotic at best. You don't know if you're jumping from safety to a spot 100 feet off the side of a cliff. But I couldn't move Killian and I wasn't going to let him get up and hobble to a car that may or may not be there.

So we jumped.

I felt the world tingle around me as I formed the new portal. It's kind of like walking your way through a sheet of silly putty. You just have to push.

There was a split second, though, a split second when out of the corner of my eye, there was a face in the ether between the two worlds. It was a face I recognized.

It was my dad.

And then it was gone as we fell through into a dry ravine bed.

Killian landed on top of me. I didn't have the strength to push him off and he was going in and out of consciousness.

"Come on, Killian. Stay with me."

Shit, he wasn't responding. In fact, he seemed to be getting heavier and heavier.

"Come on, man. This is not cool. Wake up."

I heard rustling in the shrubs and I couldn't reach a weapon under his deadweight. I hoped to god that it was friend and not foe. Ripping open portals through sheer willpower is like doing a 10k marathon in under an hour. Pretty much impossible, and even if you could, it would probably kill you.

"Wake up, Killian," I whispered.

Chapter 30

The crashing was getting louder. I turned my head and there were some of the most blessed dark-green-tights-emerging-from-the-tall-grasses I had ever seen.

Elves. Never in my life had I been so grateful to see a pack of fucking elves. They swarmed us like medics on a battlefield. Killian was lifted and settled next to me on the ground as they checked his vitals. I saw the worried looks on the elves faces as they worked on him.

Next thing I knew, hands were on me and a red-headed gent was peering into my eyes and taking my pulse.

"How did you know we'd be here?" I asked.

"Our seer prophesied this encounter."

My mom was probably having a fit. If an elf seer had been able to figure this out, Mom probably picked up on the same vibes and was downing cup after cup of loose leaf tea to make sure we were all right. Sunday dinner was not going to be fun.

"I'm fine," I said, struggling to rise.

The elf doctor placed a soft hand upon my shoulder and pushed me down, "I beg of you, gentle lady, allow me to continue my examination."

With nothing particularly better to do at the moment, I decided to relax and let the elf do his job. He flexed my joints and felt my bones, listened to my heart and made sure my pupils were the same size.

He rinsed off my boo-boos and took a canteen from his side, sitting me up to take a sip. God. Elf ambrosia. This is how most humans find themselves indebted to the race. It's like liquid sunshine with a strawberry chocolate velvet aftertaste. I felt like I could take on the entire forces of darkness with one hand tied behind my back. I mean, I could still use a nap, but after the nap, I was pretty sure I could take them.

"Thanks," I said as he helped me to my feet.

I looked as the elves loaded Killian onto a stretcher and trotted him out into the forest. My heart did a frozen hiccup and I tried to blink back the mist in my eyes as I watched him go.

"That's my partner!" I shouted after them. "You fix him up or I will hunt down every last one of you!" I finished lamely.

I turned to the doctor, "Is he going to be okay?"

He nodded as he helped me out of the ravine, "He knew of the danger when he chose to accompany you. All is as it should be."

Damned elves and their cryptic Zen-like baloney.

"I shall accompany you to the forest entrance. We shall contact you when Killian of Greenwold has recovered."

"I can't go with him?" I asked, trying to ignore the fact I sounded like a little kid who didn't understand why she wasn't invited.

"It is forbidden," the doctor said kindly.

I'd only been to the elves' capital city once in my life. It was one of those "get to know your neighbor" diversity appreciation thingies that the government had tried. After a couple of tourists had gotten eaten by some goblins during a tour of a more seedy part of the Other Side, the project was scrapped. I was sad I wouldn't have a chance to see the elf capital again, but glad that the folks who knew best how to patch up my partner were on the job. Probably better I wasn't there to gum things up, anyhow.

As we wound our way to the entrance, I was glad that the doctor was kind enough to escort me, because I would have been lost at the second left turn at the rotting tree stump. We were about an hour into our journey, animals gallivanting about as if nothing was going on, when a red fox came charging at us. I was immediately struck with a sense that things were really, really wrong. You know, wrong beyond the fact a fox had tracked us down and started talking in regular old human speech.

"The foxes of the west wood spotted the Shadow Elves---" said the fox breathlessly.

"Shadow Elves?" I interrupted, thinking how nice it would be to not have to spend the rest of my life trying to track them down, "They're here?"

But as the doctor and the fox looked at me like I was a complete bonehead, I started getting the feeling that maybe strange things were afoot at the Circle Elf.

"Yes," confirmed the impatient fox as if he was explaining things to a kindergartener. He then turned to the doctor. I guess it was time for the grown-ups to talk. "There has been an attack. The Shadow Elves were intercepted. The queen says the jade lion has once more fallen into enemy hands. We need you, doctor."

I didn't think someone so pale could pale even more, but the doctor made a liar out of me.

"My deepest regrets that our journey to return you home must be delayed. I must see if I can be of aid," he said as he bowed to me.

Whoever attacked the Shadow Elves probably had the jade lion, which, I am pretty sure, landed this problem in my jurisdiction.

"I'm right behind you," I replied, clapping him on the shoulder.

He gave me a grateful nod and then motioned at the fox to lead on. We were soon traveling at a quick trot. A fox trot, if you will.

That heebie-jeebie feeling I really wished wasn't always so right was batting a thousand.

We arrived in the clearing and it was a slaughter. There were shadow elf bodies lying at awkward angles all over the forest floor. Blood was everywhere.

It's saying something about your foe if they were able to get a jump on a shadow elf.

Several of the regular elves were already lighting pyres and placing corpses upon them before the bodies had a chance to reanimate at some awkward moment. Looking at the necks of the Shadow Elves, no one was overreacting. It had been a massacre and every one of those poor guys had gotten fanged in the carotid. I instinctively touched my neckguard, just reassuring myself it was still in place. No one should ever have to go that way.

A tall woman with wheat colored hair stood to the side overseeing things. She wore a silver circlet on her head and the waves of power coming off of her were intense. It was the first time I had ever seen the queen of the elves and my first impression was that I wouldn't want to meet her in a cold, dark alley. She was very still as we stepped onto the battleground.

One of the elves came up to her and spoke in low tones. She gave a flick of her eye to me and I knew to hop to it.

My escort and I walked across the clearing to follow her. We stopped in front of a shadow elf propped up against a tree and it took me a second to realize he was still alive. The doc was quicker on the uptake than me. He crouched right down next to the poor guy, trying to see what he could do. The shadow elf's eyes were open, though his breath was coming in ragged gasps. His neck had been torn to shreds and the fact he hadn't bled to death already was a frickin' miracle.

I could see how the Shadow Elves got their name. His skin was olive where Killian's was fair, his hair as jet black as Killian's was blonde. His dark eyes were glazed over with pain, but he obviously had been hanging on for us to get there.

She knelt down beside him and clasped his hand in hers.

"My queen, I have failed you," he gasped.

She made a shushing noise, "You gave your life in protection of our world. It is more than anyone could ever ask, more than I have right to ever ask of a subject."

"The vampires found us... they found us yesterday and stole the jade lion. They tried to create a portal, but were unsuccessful," he said painfully. I could tell that every single word cost him. "We chased them here... we tried our best..."

So that answered who had tried punching through the boundary there in Chinatown. Vampires. Vampires in cahoots with humans in cahoots with my uncle. This was getting better and better.

"We shall get it back," promised the queen.

"You must," said the dark elf, gripping her hand, "As they were leaving... I heard one say... I heard one say they were taking it to the master's stronghold..."

The queen looked over at me and I could read the directions in her face like she had written them out on a billboard in neon spray paint.

Storm the master vampire's keep.

Steal back the jade lion.

Piece of cake.

I'd get it done before lunch.

"Tell my family..." the shadow elf coughed.

I rose and stepped away to let the poor guy have his last moments in private with the leader he had given his life for.

It was all so senseless.

But I knew that if I didn't find that jade lion, this slaughter would become the norm here and on Earth. Vampires were top carnivores. If I failed, we were all in trouble. And though I didn't know where to find a master vampire, I did know a file clerk who might.

Chapter 31

By the time I found my way out of the woods, the sun was hanging low in the sky, and I was really not keen at all about being caught in the dark. My car, unfortunately, was on Earth and I had left my purse in the church during our battle.

I had only one option and I gritted my teeth, knowing I was in for it. I crossed the street to a local pub and asked to use their phone.

"Hey Mom..." I said into the receiver, as nonchalantly as I could manage.

The tirade that came down upon my head was enough to make me consider taking my chances with the nasties that come out at night.

"Mom," I interrupted, "Can you come give me a ride? You can yell at me in the car."

I guess that was not the way to phrase things because I called the Wrath of the Unappreciated down upon my head with that one. Once she had yelled herself out, though, she was out front in a matter of minutes.

"Don't you EVER give me that kind of scare again, young lady," she scolded as I climbed in and fastened my seatbelt.

"I'm sorry, Mom. I wasn't expecting to get attacked by an army of doppelgangers."

"Well, maybe if you would hone my side of your talents a little more…"

I couldn't take it anymore and decided to play my trump card, "Mom, Mindy has the sight."

That shut her up. Thank god.

"She said she is seeing Dad," I continued.

Mom shifted sort of uncomfortably in her seat, "Well, that doesn't mean anything."

This was a first.

In the past, if Mindy or I expressed even the slightest hint of sight, Mom was acting like we were on our way to the Carnegie Hall of Seers.

"Really?" I asked.

"It was probably just her missing him," she went on and then was awkwardly quiet.

That got my senses all a tingle, "But Mom… um… Here's the thing. When I was jumping through the portal, I thought I saw him, too."

"You saw nothing," she snapped.

This was a different kind of anger. Yes, she bickered and yelled, but it was all out of love. This was her slamming the door shut and I didn't know what to make of it. This was the woman who had spent lonely nights convincing herself Dad was coming back, but now the combat boot was on the other foot.

"Okay," I replied slowly, "we were probably mistaken."

We rode in uncomfortable silence all the way to my house.

"Do you have your keys?" she asked as I got out.

"Yah," I said. I had a hidden pair tucked inside a pile of fake cat poop in the garden.

She nodded primly and pursed her lips, "I don't want you to die anytime soon, do you hear me?"

I have to say that I totally agreed.

"I'll try my best not to," I replied. I shut the door and waved at her as she left.

As I walked up the path, I flipped the conversation around in my head. This was a weird day. And coming from me, that was saying something.

Chapter 32

I stumbled towards the stairs to blindly make my way to the coffee pot, but the smell of beans already brewing made a tiny little corner of my heart leap with joy.

Standing there in the kitchen, intently watching the java perk, was Killian and he was looking fit as a fiddle. I couldn't believe it.

I'm not much for displays of physical affection, but I went over to the big lug and hugged him tightly. And then socked him in the arm, "Don't you ever scare me like that again."

He put me in a headlock and gave me a knuckle sandwich, "Your wish is my command."

The elf was definitely loosening up.

I rolled out of the hold and pretty much breathed for the first time since I saw them carry him off on that stretcher.

Christ. I couldn't take it. I went over to the cupboard and grabbed some cups. "Shouldn't you be laid up for a couple more days?" I asked.

Killian rotated his arm in his cuff ruefully, "I

ache, but elves have the benefit of magical healing. So, I am back."

"Don't think I'm picking up any of your slack, Mr. Slacker McInjured Pants."

"Even half dead, I vanquished more doppelgangers than you."

"And here I thought I had finally gotten rid of you," I sighed.

"I am afraid you are stuck with me," he said as he poured himself some cereal.

I shook my head wistfully, "Maybe someday if I dream hard enough..."

Crunching his granola bits, he asked, "So, how shall we try to die today?"

While he seemed all patched up, I rested my hand on his shoulder seriously, "Are you sure you don't want to be injured a couple more days? I could use the snow break."

Killian shook his head, "We do not have time."

It sucked to be in charge of making sure there was no rest for the wicked.

"Well, I need to figure out how the heck we are going to get around with my car on the wrong side of the boundary. The jump point closest to Father Killarney's church is in the middle of your elfin forest. Somewhere." I finger combed my hair, "Killian? Do you elves have a car we could borrow?"

Killian replied, "In light of my comprised state, the queen has already secured us transportation."

I couldn't even imagine what sort of incredible ride that fairy royalty would "secure". We walked outside and, yes, it was quite unimaginable.

It looked like *Chitty Chitty Bang Bang* and a Model-T had a baby, crank start and all.

"She thought it had character," Killian stated dryly.

It certainly had that. I patted his shoulder. I guess it was better than two legs or a bicycle. Marginally.

I loaded it up with my stuff and with great puffs of smoke and coughing fits, I was able to crank the engine enough to turn it over. We chugged slowly off to the courthouse and my favorite record keeper's office.

Chapter 33

I could tell that Frank was thrilled to pieces to see me. I could tell in the way he slid the deadbolt and pulled down the shades.

"Frank, I need a favor!" I said, banging on the door.

"No one is home!" he shouted back.

"That's a lie and you know it, Frank. Open up! The sooner you unlock this door and let me in, the sooner I'm gone."

There was silence.

"You know I'm not going anywhere, Frank. I will stand out here until you lock up for the day and then I will follow you home and pound on your bedroom window all night."

I heard his feet shuffling on the other side and the locks get thrown. He flung open the door without even looking at me.

"Thanks, Frank."

"Get what you need and get out."

"I need to see your files on recent vampire attacks, Frank."

He pointed over at a messy filing cabinet, papers so stuffed into the overwhelmed drawers that it didn't even close. He turned his back to me and pretended like there was something really important he needed to type.

I started pulling everything I could find for vampire misbehavior in the past couple months. By the time I was done, my arms were full with a two-foot stack.

"Frank, you're an angel. I'll bring these back."

That made him pay attention to me, "Those files are official government property! You are not removing them from---"

"You're absolutely correct, Frank. I'm not removing them. I'm taking them offsite for reproduction. You can thank me for freeing up some storage space for you. You're welcome."

"I'm not joking!"

"You're a barrel of laughs, Frank!" I said as I backed out the door before he could stop me.

Killian had kept the car running. On our way over, I made an executive decision to practice a bit more caution with the guy and I wasn't going to let him do anything dumb, like steal files from Frank, until he was back in fighting form.

He put the car into reverse and we made our getaway as I flipped through the manila folders. Gotta say this about Frank, he was a disgusting mess, but he was a filing genius. Everything I could have hoped for was right there.

"See anything interesting?" asked Killian.

"After sundown, I'd like to spend some time mapping out the locations of these attacks."

"That is the easiest slip-up in the book. Surely a master vampire would be smart enough to avoid patterns."

"He might be, but his army of hungry blood suckers are probably going to go for a meal wherever it's available. If we see some sort of a circle form, we can pretty safely guess his headquarters is smack dab in the middle of it."

"Sounds like we have an entertaining evening to look forward to."

"I gave you CPR. You owe me."

He raised his eyebrows amorously, "We could recreate the moment."

I knew he had to be feeling better.

"Too bad, bucko. You shouldn't have slept through it."

"Promise not to sleep through it if you try again."

"Killian, what would your mother say?"

"That she's so proud her little boy has grown up to be such a virile young man."

"How about we go and find out what my mother has to say?"

"Now you are just being cruel."

Chapter 34

The day was still young and while I really enjoyed the new car scent of our current ride, I needed to get back over to Earth to grab my purse. And probably let Father Killarney know that we weren't dead.

I parked our derelict rental a few blocks away from a phone booth.

I didn't like to open up unregulated portals when I didn't have to, but the legal channels weren't worth the risk. Dad and I had pinpointed a couple of safe jump spots. This particular phone booth dumped us a ways away from the church, but nothing a good healthy hike couldn't fix.

So we jumped and we walked all the way down the Sunset Strip, past the size zero models and hipster doucheboys. The door to the church was locked and I can't say that I blamed Father Killarney.

"Guess we need to try going round back," I said to Killian.

I could see Father Killarney through the windows of the rectory and knocked softly on the paned glass. I was trying not to startle him, but he jumped defensively.

He eyed me suspiciously and walked over to the door, opening it, but leaving the chain in place.

"It's just me, Father."

He was brandishing a candlestick in his hand, "How do I know you're not a ghoul or a doppelganger?"

"I'm entirely too bright for a ghoul and too cute for a doppelganger," I replied, dryly.

He lowered his candlestick and gave a low, relieved chuckle. He closed the door and I could hear him sliding the chain. When the door opened, he came over and gave me a great big bear hug.

"Gave me a fright, Maggie-girl."

"You and me both, Father."

"Glad to see you're mended, Killian," he said, giving my partner a hearty handshake.

"Fit as a fiddle," Killian grinned, and then winced having moved just a little too fast for someone who had been almost beaten to death 24-hours before. Wuss.

"We can't stay long, Father," I said. "Just here to pick up my car and my things. We got some bad news on the Other Side."

"What's that?" he asked, hesitation filling his voice. Yah, I'd probably be scared to ask, too.

"The vampires have the jade lion again and I don't think the cavalry is coming."

Father Killarney nodded his head and sighed, "When he brought me your car, Xiaoming told me that you were under attack. He also told me he dumped you out in the middle of nowhere and I'll have you know I took him to task for it."

I patted his arm, "We probably would have been in much worse shape if he hadn't been there to come to the rescue - even if it was a very cranky rescue."

Father Killarney chuckled.

I saw my purse sitting on the table and went over to pick it up, "Thank you for taking care of us."

"Now, now," he said, "I'm afraid I am in your debt for saving my church. You name what I can do to help you next."

I looked over at Killian and he motioned for me to take the lead. I jingled my keys in my hand, "Well, we think there may be a second lion... here on Earth..."

Father Killarney nodded his head, "Go on."

"We need to track it down, but don't know anything, really, about these artifacts other than what an angry old man in Chinatown told me. Any chance you have a library filled with books on ancient lost objects or know a scholar of legendary antiquities?" I said half joking.

Father Killarney rubbed the stubble of his beard thoughtfully, "Let me make a call. I know someone who might be able to help."

Chapter 35

The Getty Museum & Library is a white monolith of modern architecture perched over one of the worst freeways in LA. Accessible only by an electric tram, Killian and I sat in our silent little car, looking out at the view as we rose up the hillside.

The museum is absolutely gorgeous. You feel like you've died and gone to Buck Rogers heaven. It is several white, utopian-esque buildings made up of hundreds of square, marble slabs flown in straight from Italy. You stroll between tended gardens and sparkling fountains as you make your way from one art gallery to the next.

It's all a front.

The place was built on one of the most active magical sites in Los Angeles. The carefully laid floor plan with its perfectly spaced perpendicular lines and postmodern style is to keep the energy flowing like water in a drainage ditch instead of flash flooding all over the city. The Powers That

Be threw a couple of random paintings on the wall to keep the normies from getting suspicious and called it good enough.

But the real magic happens behind the scenes and that's where we were headed.

We made our way over to the library. It is built in a spiral shape from the top of its domed roof to a circular clay sculpture embedded in the floor of the atrium. Rumor has it that on the summer equinox, the light shines through the skylights to illuminate the bottom of the sculpture.

We were greeted by a curator/wizard who could have been Frank's long lost twin, give or take an eyeball and some general hygiene improvements.

"Bart?" I asked with my hand out to shake his.

He totally left me hanging.

"Father Killarney said I should show you around," he grunted back at me.

"We're really grateful---"

Bart cut me off, "This library is not for public use. Some of these books are irreplaceable treasures. I was told there would only be one of you."

I looked at Killian, "Father Killarney sure has a knack for surrounding himself with charismatic, helpful fellows, doesn't he..."

Killian gave me a little salute as he left, "I will

meet you outside."

Bart watched him go, as if to make sure Killian didn't double back to steal some knowledge while no one was looking.

He let out an ox-like huff when Killian was finally gone and waved for me to follow him.

We wound our way up the circular flights until we finally reached an indistinguishable row of bookshelves. From their perfectly matched spines and cloth covers, I could tell this was going to be about as entertaining as browsing law books for laughs.

"I have to leave at 5 o'clock," Bart grumbled. "Don't plan on staying any longer than that because I'm leaving. Five-oh-oh, I lock the front door."

"Thanks, Bart. You're a peach," I replied, dryly.

I grabbed the first book entitled *China: A Complete History through Time* and started flipping pages.

Many, many, MANY hours and bookshelves later, I found something.

It was in a little, fictional book with a faded cloth cover. The book jacket was probably lost last century, but there it was – mention of a jade and diamond lion and the possibility of inter-dimensional travel.

So the two lions - one was to be rightfully stored on Earth, one on the "Other Earth", which I knew to mean the Other Side. There was a little black and white etching of the lions, along with some squiggly notations on size and identifying marks.

I looked at the diamond lion and read the caption, "Last known protector, Father Juniper Serra."

I thought back to the day that my dad disappeared. We had traveled out to Mission San Gabriel, which is this historic adobe compound built by Father Serra, the Spanish missionary largely responsible for settling California right around the same time the east coast was putting together its Bill of Rights.

My dad and I hadn't found our skips that day. There were rumors these ogres were posing as taco cart vendors and pushing street meat that even the undead wouldn't touch. But they were gone by the time we got there, so we decided to kick back a little and walk around the gardens.

Dad had excused himself to take a leak, but when he came back, he was carrying a bag from the gift shop. He said that it was just a little present for Mom. The bag had been torn and this thing that looked like a rounded shard of quartz had been sticking out of the bottom. I had teased my dad that Mom didn't need to start collecting crystals. He had laughed, but I remember him putting his hand over the hole so that no one else would see.

I looked back at the etching of the diamond lion.

What if he had been carrying the statue? What if he had found it and was trying to get it somewhere safe, not knowing that the lions couldn't travel between worlds? What if the lion had been sitting in the mission's museum collections and no one had ever noticed?

Had Dad known? Had he known that if he took it into the boundary, it would collapse on him?

I felt a chill run up and down my spine.

I flipped the pages and suddenly found a bookmark.

Written in a hand that I recognized, it said, "Don't look for me, Maggie-girl."

I held that bookmark and stared at it in disbelief. It was like my dad had come back from the grave and there he was, right in front of me, knowing that I would eventually end up looking through this book.

He had known.

He knew he would die.

Chapter 36

I replaced the book on the shelf and walked out the library to the courtyard. It was hard to tell if the gray air rolling in from the ocean was fog or smog.

I found Killian by a coffee cart on the patio. He sat at an umbrella covered table by a fountain, its water flowed into a stream that ran flush with the walkway. He handed me a cup of scalding joe. He was drinking tea with what, from the number of swizzle sticks in his cup, was probably more honey than liquid.

I took off the lid to my drink and blew at the top, testing it gingerly before I took the first swig.

"Find anything?" he asked.

"Yah," I said.

We sat for a few more moments in silence.

"Care to elaborate?" he asked.

I put down the coffee, "I think I know where the diamond lion might be."

"In an underground lock box bunker that is

impossible to get into?" asked Killian.

If only it was that easy.

"I think my dad found the lion at one of the missions."

Killian put down his drink, "It is at one of the missions? This is wonderful! We should leave immediately!"

"No, Killian," I replied, slowing him down. "What I'm trying to say is that's where it was, but my dad already found it. And I think he tried to take it to the Other Side."

"But Xiaoming said you cannot take it across..." Killian said, suddenly GETTING it. I sort of felt the same way.

"I think he knew that if my uncle found it, our family was dead. I think Dad tried to take the lion across the boundary to save us. But I think he got stuck."

Killian reached out and took my hand, "I am sorry..."

"The thing is..." I continued, trying to freeze frame the memory of a slippery image in my head, "when you were injured, I had to rip open a portal. It wasn't neat and tidy. It was sort of like a tear instead of an incision. When we went through, though, I thought I saw something out of the corner of my eye. I thought..."

Killian leaned forward.

"I thought I saw a face. Just for a moment."

"You think you saw your father..." Killian said, slowly.

"Yah," I replied. It hung in the air there for a bit, Killian looking at me and me looking at him, but he didn't make a move to call the little white men in the little white suits, so I laid out my newly evolving theory. "My sister told me that she thought she'd seen him, too, and my mom went all weird on me when I told her about it. I'm starting to think maybe my sister didn't suddenly come down with 'the sight'... I'm starting to think she's actually been seeing him."

"You think he is trapped there?"

"I think he went into hiding there."

I pulled out the bookmark. Yes, I lifted it from the library. Bart shouldn't have left me unattended, "I found this. It was in the book that told me about the statues. I think my dad knew that there would be no place safe here on Earth or the Other Side. I think he knew that my uncle would stop at nothing to control the boundary. I think my dad chose a self appointed exile inside the border with the diamond lion to save us."

I could see the wheels of Killian's mind starting to spin and put the pieces together like my mind had done. He slowly began to nod, which was much better than backing slowly away from me and calling me nutters. Killian looked up at me,

"Your theory answers many questions."

I shook my head. I suddenly had a very sick feeling in the pit of my stomach. There was something wrong and all my instincts were screaming at me.

"I think I need to go see my mom," I said, pushing down an overwhelming feeling of panic. "I think I need to go right now."

Chapter 37

I resisted laying on my horn as a speeding hearse almost knocked off my side view mirror. Asshole funeral directors.

We left my car on Earth because of that damned official portal and the fact it was probably being watched.   My illegal portal wasn't big enough for a Honda, no matter how compact, but as long as I could get to my car when I needed it without marching all over LA, I was a happy camper. And that was easy enough. I parked it by the phone booth, we climbed through dimensions, and hopped back into our waiting elfin jalopy.

I was crawling out of my skin, though.   I hadn't filled Killian in on my senseless feeling of dread, almost superstitiously believing that if I didn't say it out loud, it wouldn't come true.

I wished to god that it had just been my overactive imagination.

Unfortunately, I was my mother's daughter and her gift was one of sight and premonition.

We arrived at my mom's house and the front door was ajar.

I had my gun in my hand before I even had the car parked.

"Something wrong?"

I nodded at the door. A shadow fell upon Killian's face. He was shoulder to shoulder with me from the moment my feet hit the walkway. His staff was out and at the ready. We swept up the side of the house and flanked the front door. I pushed it open with a toe. There wasn't a sound.

Cautiously we entered. All the lights were off and there was no one home. Everything seemed in perfect order. And then I saw the note, a parchment envelope leaning on the fireplace mantel with my name on it. I picked it up and broke the red wax seal.

> *You are cordially invited to a welcome home party hosted by my dear friend, Master Vaclav. Time and location to be announced. He will be taking good care of your mother until then. An excellent housewarming gift would be a diamond lion statue.*

With great affection,
Your Uncle Ulrich.

P.S. I'm back.

Chapter 38

I put my hands on my thighs and tried to breathe in deep gulps of air. Little stars were swimming before my eyeballs. It felt like a punch to the gut. Like a great big vise was squeezing my adrenal glands and causing my heart to beat at fifty times the rate it was supposed to.

Mom.

My uncle had made it through.

And he had her.

Killian had left my side and came back with a paper bag. He handed it to me and I placed it over my mouth and nose, trying to focus on inhaling regularly. I know he was rubbing my back and stroking my hair in a comforting manner.

Next thing I know, I'm staring up at him and he's smacking my face, saying, "Wake up!"

"I'm awake!" I muttered. "I'm awake."

It took me a second to figure out where I was and what was going on, but then it came rushing back with Technicolor clarity.

"No..." I began to cry, "No..."

Killian gathered me up in to his arms and held me there against his chest as I wept, seemingly unaffected by the snot bubbles coming out of my nose and streams of water leaking out of my eyes.

"We will get her back," he murmured. "We will get her back."

Slowly I was able to pull myself together. I wiped my face on the back of my sleeve and looked at Killian apologetically, "Sorry about your shirt."

He laughed and brushed back a sweaty hair from my blotchy red face, "I shall run a load of laundry before we kick the bad guys' asses."

I hiccupped out a laugh, "Wouldn't want to get your shirt dirtied up before it got vampire guts all over it."

He gave me another hug, "You are going to be okay."

I gave him a nod. I wasn't, but I was as okay as I was going to be under present conditions.

He helped me up to my feet. I had a banger of a headache.

"Get cleaned up. See if anything comes to you. I will look around for clues."

I opened my mouth to protest, but he turned me around and pushed me towards my mom's over-decorated guest bathroom, "No arguments. Go. You are of no use to me like this."

I gave him a grateful smile and he kissed me on the top of my head, "Go."

I ran the cold water and hoped that it would chase the red from my face and eyes. I leaned my hands against the side of the sink and tried not to think about the fact my mom might be getting tortured or killed or turned at that moment.

How could she have not seen this coming?

I needed to calm down. I was going to become sloppy and miss something important if I didn't get my emotions under wrap. I splashed the water on my face.

Uncle Ulrich made it across the border somehow. Yet despite the fact that he finally made it, despite the fact he had my mom, he still wanted that damned diamond lion.

And unfortunately, he and the vampires were under the false belief that I had it. Even more unfortunate, Dad had taken that lion and I couldn't get it back.

I started to shiver and it wasn't from the cold.

I slammed off the water. The more I thought, the pissier I got.

How dare they? They made me leave Earth. They took my dad away from me. They destroyed my family. Now they had my mom. I started getting so angry I was shaking.

Mad was better.

Mad I could use.

Mad made me want to punch someone in the nose and right now all that ire was aimed at a guy whose name began with "U" and rhymed with "Ulrich".

I grabbed a clean towel off of the rack. It smelled of rose soap.

"I swear I'll find you," I vowed to any gods who might be listening.

I was my mother's daughter and I wouldn't rest until I got her back. Any undead being that thought they could get away with something like this obviously didn't know the women in my family.

Chapter 39

When I emerged, Killian was busy loading up a bunch of my mom's spice jars into a grocery bag.

"You ready?" he asked, looking up.

"Yah," I replied.

He grabbed the clanking bag and followed me outside.

I shut the door behind us, promising that the next person to open it would be my mom.

We got into the car and drove to my place. I brought in the manila folders about the vampire attacks and pulled a bunch of maps out of the back of my coat closet. Within minutes, I had a war room set up on my dining table, the local area laid out like a game of Stratego. I was so focused, even my cat knew not to come sit in the middle of my work.

Killian disappeared into the kitchen with his bag. I heard him rattling around, but it wasn't until I smelled something positively awful in the air about an hour later that I went in to see what he was up to.

My mom's jars with their curlicue labels were all over the counter. Killian was putting a pinch of this and a sprinkle of that into the little Pyrex glass bowl I usually reserved for salsa or nuking eggs.

I was never really good with potions or magic. Across the board, my life skills pretty much end at "innate ability". I can barely bake a cake from start to finish without screwing something up. The first of any recipe always turns out great because I follow the steps word for word. But after that, I like to pretend I am a master chef who doesn't need a stinking cookbook. It never ends well.

I made the decision that if I couldn't work some sensory magic with a little flour and eggs, I was categorically banned from experimenting with ingredients that could actually mess up something important.

Killian's mixture slowly began to glow.

He turned to me, "May I borrow your hand?"

He took me by the wrist and picked up a sewing needle.

"Whoa! Whoa! Whoa! I am not cool with black magic there, bucko!" I said pulling back.

He shook his head, "It is not. Uncle Ulrich's invitation will let the magic know who we want to find, but we need to let the magic know that you are the seeker."

If I wasn't looking for my mom, my answer would have consisted of two words, one being "no" and the other beginning with the letter "f", but since it was my mom, I held out my arm. I looked up at the ceiling while he poked me and squeezed out three drops into the potion.

He rotated my hand so that it was now palm down and dipped my fingers into the mix. He muttered something in elfish and then used my hand like a paintbrush across the ransom note. I left trails of light with every stroke.

When every last bit had been covered on the page, he let go of my hand.

Killian laid the note out on my dish drainer, "It has been spelled with light to find your mother. When we are facing the right way, it will glow brighter. When we are faced the wrong way, it will dim. We just need a general area to get started."

"We're playing 'Hotter/Colder' with my mom's life?"

"Yes."

At least he was telling it to me straight. I stuck my finger in my mouth to stop the blood with my tongue and waved Killian into the dining room.

I motioned to the map, "It looks like we have a concentration of attacks close to the eastern border."

Killian looked over my shoulder and traced the roads we needed to follow to get there, "Do you believe we should leave before dark?"

"I don't think we can afford to wait."

He didn't have to say a word for me to know he agreed.

Chapter 40

Yah, we headed in the right direction all right. We had driven through the night, guided by the glow of Uncle Ulrich's macabre party invitation. The road wound out of the city and into the countryside.

As the sun began to rise, we drove into a tiny village town hunkered down at the base of a completely sinister mountain. It was a quaint little place with thatched buildings and Tudor styled architecture. It even had a little fountain in the cobblestoned square. But every eave was covered in garlic bulbs and flowerbeds had been replaced with stakes poking out of the ground for easy access.

I pulled our now not-so-out-of-place car in front of an inn. The windows were shuttered and the doors locked.

"Looks like they might have had some experience with vampire types," I muttered as I stepped out of the car.

"Your keen observational skills would put a Dark Elf to shame," replied Killian dryly, his eyes scanning the sky for trouble.

I pulled a crossbow out of the trunk and strapped it to my back, "I think I deserve a raise."

"Done," said Killian.

The door to the inn opened and the proprietor cautiously stuck his head out, white horseshoe hair sticking up like he had just rolled out of bed. He startled at the sight of Killian and me. He might have been old, but before I could even twitch, he had a crossbow aimed at my heart with the safety off. I mean, I know after our all night journey we probably looked like hell, but that doesn't mean we were actually FROM hell.

I put my hands up, "Just travelers."

"Many say that," he stated matter-of-factly, "but you were here before sunrise."

"That's true..."

"I'll need you to take a drink from the fountain," he said, motioning to font in the center of town.

I lowered my hands a little and looked at him skeptically, "Now, I don't have much room to argue, because you've got an arrow pointed at my heart, but do you mind me asking why?"

"It's full of holy water. If you are a creature of darkness, you'll not be able to touch it."

The fountain was hewn from stone and the

clean looking water bubbled softly from terraced level to terraced level, but I could see that the original design had been altered to feature religious symbols and wards.

"It's not poison to people?" I asked.

"Not to people," he said.

The innkeeper gave me the room to make up my mind, but I could see he wasn't going to budge. I was going to drink or I was going to die and he was fine with whatever I decided. I gave Killian a shrug, "Shall we get on with it? I'm a little thirsty."

He looked at the fountain, "We do not appear to have much choice."

He and I walked over and stood at the edge for a moment. Man, I hoped it wasn't some spelled potion that was going to turn us into mud statues or something. In unison, we dipped our hands into it and raised the liquid to our lips.

Water. It was just plain, old-fashioned, holy water.

I actually reached down and scooped up another handful.

We turned back to the innkeeper. He had lowered his crossbow and walked over to us with his hand out, "My name's Gus. I apologize. We can't be too careful around here anymore, not since the vampires moved into the mountains. We can't even trust the sun to reveal the dark ones. It is a sorry day that I should have to greet weary travelers in such a manner."

I took his hand and shook it, "We understand completely. This is Killian, I'm Maggie."

"An elf come all this way?" asked Gus, noting Killian's ears.

"An elf and a tracker," I replied. "We have had our own fair share of scuffles with vampires. In fact, they are the reason we're here."

"You're not in cahoots with them, are you?" asked Gus, his friendly manner turning a little cautiously frosty. This guy had a hair trigger suspicion button just waiting to be pushed.

"They kidnapped my mother," I said. "We're here to get her back."

"Your mum," said the innkeeper, rubbing his jowls and shaking his head, "I'm afraid you'll need all the help you can get."

"Tell me about it."

"If you can follow me across my threshold without an invitation, I'll have some breakfast for you and a place where you can put your feet up. There's not many of us here, but we do what we can, and any enemy of our enemy is a friend of ours."

Chapter 41

We were comfortably tucked in at the table as Gus placed plates heaped with scrambled eggs and skillet potatoes before us. I'd never been so hungry in my entire life.

He sat down as we ate and started unfolding a brief accounting of recent local vampire lore.

"They moved in about six months ago. Took over the ruins of an old fortress up the mountainside a bit. Used to be a stronghold for other demon types. It had been abandoned for decades, but they had it good as new practically overnight. They remind me of wasps building a paper hive. It's a terrible place, vampires flying in and out of it at all hours. Folks say that the new master is a creature named Vaclav. They tried to create trouble when they first came, but they've left us well enough alone now that they understand we won't be caught unawares."

He jerked his thumb to some rather nasty looking weaponry hanging next to every single door, window, and fireplace in the inn. I certainly wouldn't want to run into this guy on a dark and stormy night.

"Grabbed a couple kids in those first days. I don't know much, but I'm smart enough to know you don't go pissing off a mother if you want to last on this Side. Older vampires would have known, but these were young ones, recently formed, hungry and dumb. We got 'em the next night they tried to come back. A few tried to come back for revenge. We got them, too."

I threw down my fork, "Well, they're about to discover they're not going to last very long on this Side if they go pissing off daughters, too." I looked over at Killian, "We need to hit them during the day when their strength is weakest."

Gus held up his hands, "Now, now. You're not speaking of storming that fortress all by yourselves there, lassie..."

"Oh, that is precisely what she is speaking of," replied Killian.

"I've got to," I said to Gus. "They've got my mom."

"You won't last ten minutes," he warned, wagging his finger at me, "Believe you me, there has been many a traveler come to take those creatures down, but none came back. I can't let you go in there guns blazing. Your poor mother would never forgive me."

"What would you suggest?" I asked, being smart enough to listen when someone older and wiser than me told me I was a dumbass.

"Let me loan you some horses. Your car would be limping along with busted tires before you got around the second bend. I can draw you a map. You'll also need some disguises..."

"If you can furnish us with appropriate garb, I can take care of the rest," said Killian.

I looked at him in surprise.

"Fairy glamour. It is not just for seducing the ladies," he replied.

Naturally.

"Okay, Gus. We've got some fairy glamour and some horses. What else?" I asked.

"I assume you're armed?"

"To the teeth." I paused as Killian and Gus looked at me, "No pun intended."

"Then all you need is my good wishes," said Gus as he pushed himself up from the table. "You're lucky you're going in now. The sky was dark with vampires flying out yesterday. I would suggest getting this rescue done before they return."

"Well, nothing like a deadline to get me motivated," I paused again. "No pun..."

Gus just cut me off, "I'll make sure there are clean linens on the beds for when you return."

"Plan for three guests," I replied, giving him a firm handshake to seal the deal.

Chapter 42

The monstrosity of a castle hung on the side of a cliff. It was like if a boulder and a gorilla got together and had a squat, fat baby building. Even though the afternoon sun was high in the sky, the entire place was shrouded in an unnatural gloom that made my skin crawl - as they say, the better to eat you with, my dear.

We had left our horses hitched up the road while we wandered to the overlook for this little reconnaissance/stalling mission. Normal vampires would have just transformed into bats and then flown to the castle, but our disguises weren't that good. I hoped they would accept that we were out-of- towners in for a visit.

"Killian, this was a really dumb idea and I'm thinking I would like to reconsider the plan."

He patted me firmly on the shoulder, "I am sure this is not the first time this castle has been stormed."

"Do you think anyone ever won?"

"They were all probably eaten alive at the following new moon banquet."

"Peachy," I replied.

Killian gave me a smile, "The advantage we have is that we are not storming the castle."

"Man, I hope they don't figure out that we're here..." I said, staring up at the dark parapets as shadowy figures paced between the towers.

"Our disguises should protect us."

Killian's outfit sure had me fooled. If I hadn't known it was him, I would have been looking for something stake-like right about now. His wavy blonde hair had been replaced by a shiny black mane that would put a Geisha to shame. His teeth were ever so pointy and his eyeballs had that eerie red glint to them that made my stomach clench in a whole "kill or be killed" sort of way.

"Want to know a secret?" I asked.

"Yes."

"You're totally creeping me out."

He smiled at me, "The feeling is mutual."

I was now a blondie with an alabaster undead pallor. My jeans and t-shirt had been replaced by a Victorian style riding frock in stylish black lace and swaths of material, perfect for protecting sensitive skin from the sun, from neck to toe. A dandy little top hat was perched upon my pile of Gibson curls. I flicked the black veil back over my face with a black-gloved hand and climbed the path back over to the main road to continue our ride to the castle.

Horses don't particularly enjoy hanging out amongst the damned, but these were two work nags. They had obviously seen worse and I'm sure would use the story of "that time we carried two crazy people into the heart of the vampires' lair" to entertain the other barnyard animals for years.

Killian looked over at me and I mustered up a little "here goes nuthin" spirit. I can't say that I was particularly saddened that our horses were dragging their feet.

But unfortunately, we eventually did arrive at the castle. Our mounts' hooves clomped hollowly across the drawbridge and into the covered courtyard of the keep.

The place was deserted one minute and then, in a rustle of wings, we were surrounded by a pretty serious crowd of vampire guards the next.

I looked over at our menacing welcome party with what I hoped was a haughty expression.

"State your business," hissed a weaselly little vampire with bad skin. His head was totally level with my foot and I fantasized bashing in those man-eating teeth with the toe of my dainty little shoe.

"How dare you even ask," Killian replied as he vaulted off of his horse and came over to offer me his hand.

"You are trespassing..."

"We bear important news for the master," I snapped back at him.

The group hissed at me as they writhed in a seething attack formation.

"Don't make me bite you, young one," I said as I removed my gloves finger by finger. "You will attend to our horses. You will give us room to rest. And then you will bring us to your master."

"And why should I do that?" he replied.

I leaned in close so that he could see I meant business. I could even feel my fangs lengthen and, judging from the way his eyes widened, I guess it was kinda scary effective.

"Because I can walk in daylight," I replied.

Well, that just set the group of little bloodsucking bastards off into a tizzy. Killian handed one of them the reins to our mounts.

"Don't eat them," I called out. "We want them for later."

The vampires hissed with laughter. Oh, funny funny with the eating horses humor. Dumb vampires.

We followed the weaselly one into the castle. He led us up some stone staircases and down hallways. We passed truly gruesome artwork that some sicko decided was worthy of being preserved forever in oil and canvas and framed in gold gilt. I was almost thankful when the weaselly one piped up to express what was weighing heavily upon his twisted little heart.

"Our master will be most anxious to meet with you," he said. "He is not here, but we will send out a messenger as soon as night falls. You should rest. You could give me the object that allows you to walk in daylight, and I could keep it in a safe place."

I gave him a smile, "You are so helpful. Do you want the object?"

He leaned forward as Killian rolled his eyes, knowing where I was going.

"This is what lets me walk in sunlight." I pulled out my stake, "It is called 'mortality'."

And with that, I nailed him clean through the heart.

As the vampire fell, Killian shook his head, "Did you have to blow our cover quite so soon?"

"It was only going to get more difficult to get rid of him from here on in," I replied. "Grab an end."

Killian dutifully walked over to the other side and helped me shove the corpse behind a tapestry. I hoped the cleaning crew wouldn't be in until morning and all of the other vampire guests were too snooty to bother themselves with the world's largest undead dust bunny.

I wiped my hands off on my velvet skirts as I scanned the hallway, "Now, if I were a master vampire, where would I hide a jade lion?"

And then something clicked in my head. It was like my nose was a magnet and I suddenly could feel north.

"It's this way," I said, grabbing Killian's arm and walking him swiftly down the hall. God bless my family's gift, I was better than a bloodhound.

We didn't get too far before I saw some vampire shadows on the wall moving quickly in our general direction. I shoved Killian into a doorway and planted my wrist on his lips before he could ask what the hell I was doing. I leaned against him like he was making an enjoyable meal out of me. I let my lids half close and my eyes glaze over as an elegantly dressed couple passed by. They smiled in warm approval, as if to say, "Ah, I remember the days of opening up my beloved's arteries and sucking out her vital fluids."

As soon as they passed I pulled away, but Killian wrapped an arm around my waist and drew me back with a twinkle in his eye.

"We don't have time for this---" I protested.

He shut my lips with a wrist to my mouth and went slack, leaning his head upon my shoulder. I gave a little finger wave to a second couple that passed by. They seemed like maybe they were a little less nostalgic about the good old days. She gave her escort a glare and I knew someone was in for it tonight. Killian felt me relax as soon as they were out of view.

"We always have time for this," he whispered and planted a kiss beneath my ear. He then grabbed my hand and pulled me out into the hallway. "Which way?" he asked.

Fucking elves.

I let the focus settle back into my bones and we were off to the races again. There seemed to be a general pattern of "down" to our direction. Down hallways... down staircases... Whenever we could duck from sight we did, but it seemed like most of the vampires were more interested in getting where they were going and not standing around making idle chitchat with their fellow damned.

Finally, we came to a bolted door with big metal bands and spiky things. That homing instinct was screaming at me that we needed to get through it.

"Okay, Killian, you're up."

He recoiled from the door. "I cannot touch it," he replied.

"What are you talking-" and then it hit me. Cold iron. The entire door was made up of cold iron – perfect for keeping the fairies at bay. Hopefully, the master had banked upon the probability that a human would never have made it this far.

I opened up my purse and pulled out a little lock pick set. I inserted the metal doohickeys into the locks and fiddled around until I felt the blessed little click of the tumblers all falling into their proper place.

I pushed open the door and waited silently in case some monster was hanging around to rush us.

There wasn't a sound, so I waved at Killian to follow me. The place was pitch black. Killian rested his hand upon my arm and I waited to see what nifty little trick he had up his sleeve.

"Night-blooming shade charm," he whispered. He slipped a ring upon my finger and the hallway was suddenly lit in an eerie green glow. "The light is only visible to the wearer."

I nodded at him, impressed. He totally made up for the boondoggle at the iron door.

I especially thanked him as I saw four vampires sprinting towards us silently. If we had been creeping along in the dark, Killian and I would have been human shish kabobs in a hot minute.

Instead, I had enough time to reach up my sleeve and pull out my stakes before they attacked. I braced as they left the ground to fly at me and with a pop-pop, they were skewered before they hit the floor. I turned and Killian had dispatched the other two.

Single file, we crept along the shadows and hugged the walls. The sense of drawing continued to whisper its sweet song to me and, unerring, Killian and I continued our way down into the heart of the castle.

We encountered a couple more bands of soldiers, but dispatched them in short order. My dress was getting gunky from the carnage and I felt like I would never really ever get clean again.

And then we came to the door.

It was a massive thing - iron, again. I was on my own. I looked for the lock and realized there was none.

Instead, there was a door handle with a nasty looking spike where your thumb would normally go.

I stood there for a moment and tried not to lose my lunch. I had heard about doors like this. Magical. Impenetrable. The only thing that would get that door to open was blood and the iron suggested the door didn't want fairy blood. Which left human blood.

I placed my thumb on the latch and it poked me like a rose thorn. A big, fat droplet of blood ran down the metal spike.

And the door swung open.

Chapter 43

The room was dark. A desk sat at one end upon a really expensive carpet, probably stolen from some rich guy eaten centuries ago. The walls were lined with shelves and books. Sitting on a pedestal in a plaster niche lit like something out of a gawdamned movie was the jade lion.

Killian stood next to me as we stared at it in silence.

It was the size of a pint glass, absolutely unremarkable to look at. It could have been mistaken for a Chinatown souvenir. But, man, there was a glow whenever I looked at that thing. It was radiating green like someone had turned on a porch light to welcome me home.

More minutes passed as Killian and I looked at it.

"This is such a trap," I said.

"Yes."

"There is no way that they would leave this thing so weakly protected."

"No," Killian said as he gave me a slow smile

and walked over to the statue, do or die. He picked it up gingerly, as if waiting for some siren to go off or a cage to descend, but neither happened.

Instead, he just lifted it up, and then slowly walked back towards me.

"I say we go home," he offered.

But that's when the shift happened. Or the alignment.

As soon as Killian was standing next to me with that jade lion's eyes facing the same way as my eyes, the wall between the worlds opened up like an automatic door at a discount shopping center.

I had never felt anything so easy.

One minute, I was looking at Vaclav's library shelves. The next, I was staring through a portal at the psychedelic painted buildings and swaying palm trees of Venice Beach.

I stepped into the portal, but instead of the paper thinness I usually felt in the border, it was like a glitter tunnel of rainbow lights. Just this one lion was able to harmonize with my innate talent and hold the portal with a stability that I never experienced on my own. I felt my vampire disguise melt away and my true self return.

I stood in this bubble between the two worlds.

"It's strange," said Killian. "I can see right

through you."

I let myself sink into the other time-ness of this middle dimension. I kept my eyes towards the gardens, but rather than moving forward, I stuck my hand out to the side.

And felt fingers grasp mine.

I put a foot in front of me and stepped over to Earth. It felt like I was pushing through mud. I did not let go of that hand.

I strained against the great vacuum trying to pull him back into the middle dimension. Sweat prickled on my brow.

"Keep going, Maggie. You have almost got him!"

And then suddenly, we were out. I turned. Standing there almost glowing in the California sun was my dad. He looked haggard and worn. But it was him.

And in his hand was the diamond lion.

Chapter 44

"Maggie-girl?" his hands went to my face, as if unable to believe it was really me.

"Dad?"

"I didn't know if you would ever know what had happened..."

Killian cleared his throat, "Should I come over?"

And then there was a sound in the Other Side office. I turned and saw a guy who looked eerily like a younger version of my dad step through the door.

"Ulrich..." my dad hoarsely whispered.

"I think you should stay!" Ulrich roared.

I screamed, "Killian, come through!"

A blast shattered across the room and hit Killian, knocking him to the ground. But Killian didn't let go of the jade lion and the statue's gaze held open the portal.

"Dad?" I asked, turning to him.

Dad was no match for Ulrich right now. We both knew it. This was going to have to be my fight.

"Dad, I'll be right back..."

Dad saw the resolve in my eyes and smiled, "That's my Maggie-girl."

He lifted the diamond lion. Energy crackled across the portal as its power connected across dimensions with the jade lion. He gave me a nod and I jumped through to the Other Side.

Uncle Ulrich laughed as he saw me come through, "Well, well, well. If it isn't my long lost niece. I had such hopes for you..."

"Where is my mom?" I asked as I pulled my sai out of my boot tops.

"You mean that animal your father lay with?"

"Come on. That's my mom you're talking about," I said.

Uncle Ulrich pulled a sword down from the wall, "Really, if you've come to fight your mighty uncle, you could have done better than those little blades."

"Yah, well, I wasn't planning on this being the final showdown. How did you get across?"

"My dear Maggie, it turns out that when you slaughter a room full of enough humans, you can gather enough energy to harmonize with the jade lion. It is awfully messy and inconvenient, though, so if you'll just hand over the diamond lion, we can both go on with our separate lives."

"I'm afraid that I can't do that," I replied.

"Then I'm afraid I will have to kill you."

"No really, even if I wanted to, I couldn't give it to you."

"You are repeating yourself."

"I'm trying to tell you something, jerkface!"

We circled each other in that small room, stepping carefully over Killian. Uncle Ulrich's eyes squinted with hate when he saw who was standing on the other side of the border.

Dad gave him a weary little wave, "Good to see you again, brother."

"I'm so pleased you'll be here to witness me destroy your daughter," said Ulrich as he attacked.

The clang of his sword against my sai sent shocks up my arm. I really should have brought a bigger knife. But the worst part was that the metal in my hand started to heat up. I jerked myself away.

"OW! Magic? Really?"

My uncle let out an evil laugh.

"And with the laughing...?" I said. Seriously, I would be doing the world a favor getting rid of this guy just for the maniacal cackling. He was like a frickin' cartoon.

Unfortunately, he bounced back like a cartoon character, too, no matter how many anvils you dropped on his head.

I saw my dad twitch forward to try to come

to my rescue and I shouted back, "Dad! No! Keep the portal open!"

While I was distracted, Uncle was able to slash me across the upper arm.

There's this thing about getting cut with a sword. You don't feel it for a second and then you see the blood and it hits you that hey, I've been cut with a sword.

And then little black and white dots start floating in front of your eyes from all of the nerve endings getting sliced.

"A little flesh wound is going to stop the mighty Maggie?" he taunted.

What an asshole. I had been on the giving end of such treatment, but the receiving end was a different matter. Good thing I had two hands and two sai, because the one in my left hand wasn't working so good, which wouldn't have been such a problem if this was a pop quiz, but this was a final examination to determine whether I was going to live or bite it.

I upped my attack, blocking and jabbing with my knives. If he needed an appendectomy, now would have been a great time because I opened him up for the surgeons with a nice little cut to his paunch, no co-pay required.

Unfortunately, it just pissed him off. And that's when he started fighting dirty. A vase came flying at my head and I ducked just in time for it to miss me, watch it shatter against the wall, and turn back to Ulrich to block his incoming blade. Then a chair came sliding across the room, knocking me off my feet.

And the thing about it is that after years of scrabbling with vampires, I wasn't above playing dirty, too.

Must be genetic.

I gave him a kick right in the boo-boo that I had just given him. He clutched his side and backed up, giving me a chance to jump to my feet and attack. I wasn't about to give him a break out of sympathy. Do unto others and shit because sometimes they'll do unto you.

He seemed to be able to handle my two hands pretty good, but was completely screwed trying to block two arms and two feet. Meanwhile, I was having a devil of a time blocking all of the stuff he was causing to fly at me. I hoped to god that Killian's unconscious body wasn't getting impaled by anything too dangerous. I would have loved to have helped him out, but I was kind of overwhelmed at the moment.

The backing and forthing was relentless.

I was getting tired and I could see my uncle was, too.

And then I saw a look in his eye and knew that this was it. He was going for broke. He lifted up his sword and swung it at my neck. The sonofabitch was going to decapitate me!

I instinctually raised my sai to block the blow, but his sword came too fast.

It hit my neck with a nasty "chunk" sound.

I staggered and then fell forward, resting against Ulrich's chest. I looked up into his eyes and then pulled down the lace from my high Victorian neckline, "Neckguard."

And as I gave him an apologetic smile for having to ruin Christmas, I lifted my knee and got him square in the groin.

His sword fell to the ground as he grabbed his man package.

I gave him a slight push and he staggered back, reaching out to steady himself on the wall of the portal.

"I'll kill your father," he gasped.

Oh, the dramatics. I leaned over and picked up the jade lion.

"Hey, Uncle Ulrich! One of my greatest disappointments is that as a child, you were never there to play CATCH!"

And with that, I threw that jade lion at him.

I saw his greedy little brain practically lick its lips as he reached up and caught it. He held it over his head in triumph.

"Now Dad!" I yelled.

And Dad, after having been trapped inside

that boundary for years, knew what to do.

He turned the eyes of the diamond lion away, and there was only time for a look of "Oh SHIT" to cross Uncle Ulrich's face before the portal crashed closed on him. And since there is no up or down in nowhere, no place for that damned jade lion to face to open up any portals, he was trapped forever, ensuring us that not only would he never show his ugly mug again, but that the lion could never fall into the hands of the wrong types of people. Types like him.

I bent over, resting my hands on my thighs. They suddenly started trembling uncontrollably and I collapsed onto the ground.

I looked down at my hands, where they had been burned by my heated sai. My neckguard may have prevented my head from being lopped off, but the hit was going to leave a mark. I took a deep breath and thanked whatever effed up god lived in whatever dimension it lived in for giving me a few more days to waste jumping between worlds.

I looked over at Killian. I rolled him on to his side, "Hey kid, wake up."

He moaned and his eyelids fluttered a bit.

I gave him a shake, "Come on you faker, the danger is over."

He slowly lifted his head and winced. He was probably sporting a banger of a concussion right now.

"How you feeling?" I asked.

He lay back down on the ground, "Like I got hit by a blast of magic."

"Well, you're in luck. That's exactly how you are supposed to be feeling." I put out my hand, "Come on, we still have to go find my mom."

He nodded grimly and let me haul him to his feet. We were both limping as we made our way to the door.

"We better not run into any bad guys, because I'm liable to just let them kill me," I moaned.

We opened the door and there were two vampires.

With a grimace, I tossed Killian a sai and we both staked the bastards before they were even able to move.

"The next bad guys. The next bad guys I'm going to let kill me," I said as I yanked my sai out of the vamp's heart.

Killian wiped the goo on his trousers and returned me my improvised stake. He then went back into the room and grabbed up Ulrich's sword from the ground.

"I do not plan on doing any killing. I am just going to use this as a cane so that I do not fall over," he said.

I couldn't argue, "After you, old man."

He hobbled out.

The halls were quiet, but we tried to remain alert for any surprise attacks. We didn't find Master Vaclav and there was a noticeable decline in the undead types. I had the strangest feeling that perhaps he had some inkling how this was going to shake out and that's why he had chosen to retire to some offsite location. Still, room by room, we cleared out the few bad critters we ran into and checked to make sure that my mom wasn't chained to a wall.

When we found her, she actually was chained to a wall.

Mom looked up. Her hair was unkempt and her muumuu dirty, but she looked more put out than fearful. The moment I stepped in, she gave a huge sigh of relief and then started kvetching, "It took you so long, I wasn't even sure you would come. Your uncle showed up and he acted as if I should be bowing down before him like he was the second coming of Erik Estrada, which, I will tell you, he is not. Then he says he is going to leave a ransom note, but you really can't trust men with these sorts of things. He probably didn't even tell you where to find me. Your uncle..."

I smiled. The sound of her voice had never

been sweeter.

Killian found the keys hanging by the door on a big iron key ring and we had those manacles off of my mom's hands lickety split. I threw my arms around her, not ever wanting to let go. Teach her to scare the bejeezus outta me.

She stroked my hair, "Now, now. I'm fine. I saw this coming."

I pulled away and wiped some moisture that seemed to be leaking from my eyes, "I found Dad. He's alive and safe, just like you always knew he was."

She got very, very quiet, "Did you find the note he left you?"

I nodded.

"He knew someday that you would find out the truth. He insisted on leaving it for you. He didn't want you to put yourself in harm's way." She leaned forward and gave me an Eskimo kiss, "I'm glad you didn't listen."

"Why didn't you tell me?"

"I couldn't. Your father and I made that decision to keep you and your sister alive. He was safe and we were safe. It was all we could do."

I nodded. As I thought about the moment I had found the ransom note, of realizing Mom was missing, I understood what a person would try to do to keep their family safe.

She rubbed my back, "How does he look?"

"Like he could use some of your good cooking," I said with a smile. "You ready to go see him?"

We all trooped back up to the office and I reopened the portal. Dad was standing right there on Earth waiting for us. His eyes lit up as he saw me. I stepped through and took the diamond lion from him. He wrapped me up in his arms, but I gave him a gentle shove towards someone on the Other Side who needed him more than me at the moment.

"Mom? How about you take Dad home? I've got to make sure this gets into the right hands," I said waving the diamond lion casually.

She held out her arms and Dad stepped through the border, both of them crying and laughing like a couple of crazy kids who were just wild about each other.

"Get a room!" I shouted.

Killian cast a nifty little vampire glamour disguise on my folks as he ushered them out of the room.

But before he left, Killian turned and locked eyes with me. I gave him a little wave, "Thanks."

And then I let the portal close.

I whipped my cell phone out of my satchel, trying not to look too out of place, what with my late 19th Century garb and vampire guts and diamond statue. I punched in a text and slowly made my way across the beach.

It's funny how the most mundane situations can sometimes put things in such complete context. There were parents unloading strollers from the backs of their SUVs. Old ladies carrying umbrellas to stay out of the sun. The waves still roared. The birds still chirped. Crazy burnouts still played hacky sack. And none of them had a clue that they had just been saved from annihilation.

Nuts. The whole living thing was just nuts and I started to laugh all alone out there.

I don't know if it was life choosing that particular moment to make sure I didn't scare the children or what, but my euphoria was interrupted by my cell phone ringing.

"Hello?"

The line was silent, like it used to be back in the day when you were making an international call.

"Hello?" I asked again.

"Maggie MacKay. Magical Tracker," stated some guy whose voice made my teeth ache like nails on a chalkboard.

"Who is this?" I asked.

"My minions have reported that you were successful in disposing of your uncle."

The squirrels in my brain pushed the pieces together and you could almost hear a "clunk" as the cogs and wheels FINALLY started spinning.

"Vaclav?"

"A pleasure to finally speak with you, my dear Ms. MacKay."

"You're a dick," I said. The guy tried tearing down the border and destroying the entire human race. I wasn't in the mood for etiquette.

"Congratulations on your win, Ms. MacKay. After having spent some time with your uncle, I was quite certain he would not be a match for you," said the master vampire.

"Um... thanks?"

"But know this – enjoy your victory while you can because it shall be your last."

I sputtered into the handset, "I think that what you meant to say was that this was my first. Of many. I'm going to have so many firsts, you aren't even going to be able to count how many firsts I have kicking your..."

"Make no mistake, Ms. MacKay!" he bellowed, giving a vocal performance unheard since *Phantom* left Broadway, "The vampires shall walk in the sun once again!"

I, however, had caught that particular musical and let me just say, he was not Michael Crawford.

I pounded the "off" button and hung up on the guy.

Life is too short to waste daytime cell minutes being yelled at by a vampire.

I stretched my arms over my head and stared out at the ocean. Not bad for a day's work.

About a half hour later, my car pulled up by the boardwalk, the bitty driver barely able to see over the dashboard.

I opened up my car door and placed the diamond lion on the passenger side floor and covered it with my foil car shade.

"Thanks, Pipistrelle," I said.

He gave me a little salute, "Good news?"

"Indeed," I replied. "I have vanquished my evil uncle."

"Then my work here is done," he said wistfully. "I suppose I shall have to return to the Other Side before my permit expires."

Vaclav's phone call was sitting in my stomach like bad potato salad at a church picnic. And then I got a brilliant idea.

"Pipistrelle, would you like a new mission?"

He nodded his head, as if he couldn't believe his good luck.

"My sister lives here on Earth and I need someone to make sure she is protected. Would you be up for the task?"

He hopped on the seat excitedly, "Indeed! I'm

your brownie! Indeed!"

I nodded, "Good. Then you have yourself a job. Permanently. I'll get all the paperwork done when I get to the Other Side."

Pipistrelle jumped out of the car.

"Pipistrelle! Come back!" I shouted.

"No, Maggie, dear! I must go protect your sister's home!"

I grinned as his little hat disappeared behind a flowerbed, knowing he had found his bliss.

The drive out to Chinatown was uneventful. I found parking over on Hill Street. I walked up those long steps to Xiaoming's apartment. His lions gave me a nod as I stood there. Nice to see I got the hunks of concrete's seal of approval.

I rapped on the flimsy aluminum screen door.

Xiaoming shuffled over to me, cigarette burned down to the filter. He lit another one off the end and asked, "What you want?"

"I got you a present."

He opened up the door and ushered me in, barely giving me a glance. I took the lion out of my reusable shopping bag and set him on the table.

"Think you can get him home for me?" I asked.

Xiaoming's craggy face broke into a smile. He took the statue from the table and cradled it like a baby, "I take good care of him. Will take him home now."

He walked into the other room and was gone for several minutes. When he returned, he said, "He is safe."

And then Xiaoming gave me a deep bow, "Thank you, Maggie MacKay."

I gave him a little nod and awkwardly bunched up the empty bag. The lions guarding his door were still as I left.

I drove my car across town and wound my way up to Mulholland, rolling down my windows and letting the heat of the day wash over me.

I started reviewing the day's events: destroyed my uncle. Check. Saved my Mom and Dad. Check. Delivered ancient artifact of unknown power to a crazy Chinese guy. Check. Dinner with the family?

I looked over the rim at the Los Angeles skyline as my stomach growled.

Seemed like the perfect time to drive off a cliff.

And I gunned it.

Acknowledgements

It drives my mom to distraction when the folks accepting their Oscars thank their families last instead of first, so let's get it out on the table before I am written out of the will –thanks always and forever to my family. They have supported me through all my hair-brained schemes and let me pursue an artist's life with barely a "When are you going to get a real job?" In fact, most of the time I get a, "Wow! That's wonderful!" You have no idea how much your support of me and my last book means. Sorry about all the cussing in this one.

This book exists solely because of the internet writing community and the panic that set in when I signed up for NaNoWriMo. It is a fantastic time and you really should do it this year. No, really.

Many thanks to Matt Troyer who forced me to start blogging, where I met folks like Giddy Girlie, Bliss Blog, Styrofoam Kitty, Out of Character, Byrne Unit, Mermaid Jones, Orlith and others whose writing left me in awe. Thank you for the inspiration and giving me a glimmer of what writing could be. It was a glorious age.

Thank you to my beta readers Adam Jackman and R.B. Wood for your insight and enthusiasm. I would have burned this manuscript without you! There is a special place in heaven for those willing to plow through a first draft… Thank you to Ray Stilwell at Captainsblog for editing this mutha and all your support. You all earned your wings!

A special thanks to my Scooby Crew - Mia Winn, Ryan Winn and Adam Jackman. Thanks for being my partners in crime here in Los Angeles. I know this city because of you. Thank you for the love and adventure!

Maryland Distinguished Scholar in the Arts and twenty year veteran of stage and screen, Kate Danley received her B.S. in theatre from Towson University.

Her debut novel, The Woodcutter, was honored with the Garcia Award for the Best Fiction Book of the Year, named the 1st Place Fantasy Book in the Reader Views Literary Awards, and won the Sci-Fi/Fantasy category in the Next Generation Indie Book Awards.

Her plays have been produced in New York, Los Angeles, Washington, DC, and Baltimore. Her screenplay Fairy Blood won 1st Place in the Breckenridge Festival of Film Screenwriting Competition in the Action/Adventure Category and her screenplay American Privateer was a 2nd Round Choice in the Carl Sautter Memorial Screenwriting Competition.

Her films and shorts *The Playhouse, Dog Days, Sock Zombie, SuperPout*, and *Sports Scents* can be seen in festivals and on the internet.

She lost on Hollywood Squares.

www.katedanley.com.

Also by Kate Danley

Winner of the Garcia Award for
Best Fiction Book of the Year

1st Place Fantasy Book
Reader Views Reviewers Choice Awards

Winner of the Sci-Fi/Fantasy Category
Indie Book Awards

Available in Paperback & e-Book

Maggie MacKay
Magical Tracker Series

"If urban fantasy could be bottled, then this story is a shot-glass full of awesomesauce."
- Dark Side of the Covers

Maggie for Hire
Maggie Get Your Gun
Book Three Coming in 2013!

FROM THE AWARD WINNING AUTHOR OF
THE WOODCUTTER

5800

BREAKOUT

KATE DANLEY

A short story about escaping the office...

An ebook exclusive!

24422488R00154

Made in the USA
Lexington, KY
17 July 2013